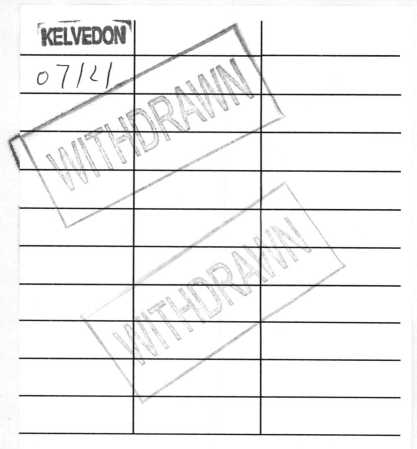

Please return this book on or before the date shown above. To renew go to www.essex.gov.uk/libraries, ring 0345 603 7628 or go to any Essex library.

Essex County Council

D0257463

Also by Mark Lowery

Charlie and Me

MARK LOWERY

Piccadilly
PRESS

First published in Great Britain in 2020 by
PICCADILLY PRESS

80–81 Wimpole St, London W1G 9RE
Owned by Bonnier Books
Sveavägen 56, Stockholm, Sweden
www.piccadillypress.co.uk

A CIP catalogue record for this book is available
from the British Library.

ISBN: 978-1-84812-737-1
Also available as an ebook

2

Designed by Perfect Bound Ltd
Printed and bound by Clays Ltd, Elcograf S.p.A.

MIX
Paper from
responsible sources
FSC® C018072

Piccadilly Press is an imprint of Bonnier Books UK
www.bonnierbooks.co.uk

For
Jim Lowery (1925–2019) and Mary Lowery,
and for S, J, S and O

OUTSIDE HEAVENLY COD FISH AND CHIP SHOP, PRESTON

Megan

I'm in the middle of a whirlpool, struggling for breath while the world swirls around me, threatening to swallow me up.

There was a *screech*. A *crunch*. A horrible, wet *thud*. I think I screamed but now I'm standing over him, frozen and numb.

The headlights of the car cast Daniel's shadow long into the road – arms and legs twisted at weird angles. His duffel coat's ridden up at the back and the skin underneath is angry, red and shiny, like it's been peeled off. Chips and bits of fish are scattered about the tarmac among the broken fragments of his magnifying glass.

Now Dad's run out of the chip shop and he's kneeling next to him, holding his hand, telling him, *Everything's going to be OK, Big D.* The driver is out of her car and hopping about. *He just ran out from nowhere. How could I have stopped?*

Mum's rushing over, barking into her mobile for an ambulance, and Grandma's hobbling behind her.

Dad clicks his fingers. 'Monkey.' His voice is shaky, urgent. He doesn't look up, so it takes me a few seconds to realise he's talking to me.

Daniel's cuddly toy monkey is lying in the gutter. The one he takes everywhere with him. The one he's had since he was a baby. Moving like I'm floating, I pick it up and wipe the grit from the permanently soggy hand that Daniel likes to suck for comfort.

Monkey is not looking good.

Its leather jacket and sunglasses are scuffed and its I HEART NEW YORK T-shirt is all dirty. Its tail's been torn off and a wisp of white stuffing hangs out of a hole in its bottom.

I hand the toy to Dad. Its arms and legs dangle limply. Without looking at me, he places it carefully next to Daniel's face and strokes his cheek. 'We're going to help you,' he says. 'You've had a little accident. Monkey's with you. And he's lost his tail, look.'

Somehow Daniel has managed to hold on to his notebook. I ease it out of his hand and put it in my pocket for safekeeping.

'Give Monkey's hand a kiss,' Dad says to him.

Daniel's eyes flicker open and, for a moment, he almost smiles. He groans, mutters something, and puts

Monkey's hand in his mouth. Then he softly closes his eyes again.

Daniel

Everything HURTS and I'm awake asleep floaty falling and bright lights. Is this the White feeling or is it the Grey? And there's something on my cheek. I open my eyes which I didn't know were shut and the WHOLE WORLD is BLURRED and SIDEWAYS and half of my face is COLD and WET and LOOK AT THAT! How did Monkey get right in front of me?

Is everything gonna be OK, Big D? Monkey croaks and this is very STRANGE and very EXCITING, what with him being a CUDDLY TOY, and isn't it funny that he's got an American accent?

Are there any chips left? I ask, but I don't know if the words even come out of my mouth, and Monkey doesn't answer, he just goes, Arghhhhh! and screws up his face, and I realise he's in PAIN and I feel Turquoise, which is guilty, because I didn't notice and I say, Monkey, what's wrong?

And he says, You gotta help me. I've been in an accident. It's my tail. Give my hand a kiss, man.

So I do and then everything goes

SIX WEEKS LATER, ROYAL PRESTON HOSPITAL

Megan

I shake myself back into the room.

Probably it's being in the hospital again that made me drift off like that. But it happens a lot: I blink and I'm back there, seeing Daniel's crumpled little body in the road.

Or I'm in a lesson and I start daydreaming about that long night spent in this same hospital we're in now. Dad pacing back and forth. Mum sipping cold coffee through pinched lips. Me sitting there, unnoticed, as doctors come and go:

'We've done the X-ray. A few bumps and bruises but no major injuries. He was lucky. Five miles an hour faster and, well...'

And, later, as grey morning light filtered in through the windows:

'Starting to wake up. Bit groggy, but he seems happy enough cuddling his toy monkey. We'll keep him in for a few days. Right as rain in no time.'

It's just over six weeks since Daniel got run over outside the chip shop.

Somehow, thankfully, he survived.

You'd look at him now and you'd think there's nothing wrong with him: no scars, no limp, no bandages, no plaster casts. Nothing. Not a scratch. The only mark is a patch of red skin on his back, which the doctors promise will fade in time.

He's had X-rays and scans. He's been sent through this tube thing that took pictures of the inside of his whole body. He's had lights shone in his eyes and electrodes stuck to his skull. You name it, they've checked it. And every single test has come back the same: no injuries. No damage to his brain. *Physically* he's fine.

But my brother is **not** fine.

The accident changed him completely.

Right as rain.

As if.

I look around the room, embarrassed. Did I say that out loud?

If I did, nobody noticed. They never do. I could paint myself purple and dance naked on my chair and Mum and Dad wouldn't raise an eyebrow.

Daniel's sitting in the corner with his knees tucked up to his chest, hiding under Dad's woolly jacket.

From underneath it, I can hear him muttering to his toy

monkey in his bizarre half-language of grunts and noises. This is how he's spent every waking hour since he got run over.

The old Daniel got vaporised the moment the car smacked into him. He's been replaced by this weird, floating zombie who doesn't speak properly, doesn't even seem to recognise us. You look into those beautiful big brown eyes and they're just dark, murky puddles.

There are three problems: nobody knows exactly **what** is wrong with him, nobody knows **why** he's like this, and nobody knows **how** to sort it out.

And they're the reasons why we're here. Again.

Mum and Dad are at the desk, talking with the psychologist or neurologist or zoologist or whatever today's specialist doctor is. I've been told to stay out of the way and keep quiet, like I'm three or something.

'Homework, Megan,' says Mum, mid-conversation, without looking over at me.

Rolling my eyes, I pull out my history book and flick past pages and pages of neat, small writing and green ticks. I grit my teeth as the writing suddenly gets bigger, scruffier, more rushed, and the ticks become red question marks, squiggly lines and increasingly snippy comments:

I expect more from you, Megan.

DID YOU READ THE NOTES? They did not have telephones in Tudor times!

Three lines is not acceptable for a whole lesson! And who is Henry the Ninth?

I can't be doing with this so I shut the book. I'll do it on the bus tomorrow.

I'm only here because I didn't want to stay home with Grandma. She moved in with us straight after the accident and we've not been able to get rid of her. She's there to 'help us out', but all she does is moan and demand cups of tea. I love her and everything, but she is SERIOUSLY annoying.

Today she's got wind. She won't admit to it though, because it's *common* and *rude*. Every time she lets one go, she tries to drown it out by pretending to cough, or by shouting out random rubbish like: 'Was that the doorbell?' or 'Biscuits. Are there any biscuits?'

I've left her home alone to fart in peace.

'But you're not answering the question,' says Mum angrily to the doctor. 'Why can't you tell us what's wrong with him?'

The doctor sighs.

If you ask me, it's obvious what's wrong with Daniel: he hasn't got over the shock of being run over.

But why would you ask me? Nobody else does.

Daniel and Monkey

Monkey and me are in our brand-new TOP-SECRET SPECIAL HIDEOUT, which is super-cool and super-warm.

— Hey, D-Man. What gives? I can't see nothing, says Monkey who's actually American from New York City so he always says things like I CAN'T SEE NOTHING and YO, PUNK, GET ME A HOT DOG, EASY ON THE ONIONS and EAT LEAD, YA FILTHY ANIMAL. I think he'd be able to see more if he took off his sunglasses, but he can't because they are sewn into the sides of his head, which must be uncomfortable and annoying.

I turn on the torch which is NICE and BRIGHT.

— That's MUCH BETTER, I say, because now we can see each other.

— Hand-wash only? Don't tumble-dry? What kinda joint ya brought me to, huh? says Monkey, looking at the ceiling of our top-secret special hideout.

— Don't worry. That's just what they write on TOP-SECRET SPECIAL HIDEOUTS these days, I say.

The roof is actually hanging down from my head

and covering my knees, which are bent so that we have space to breathe and chat but NOT MOVE. I like it because it's COSY and I can be really close to Monkey.

— Should we play I SPY? I say, which is a VERY FUNNY JOKE because all we can see is each other and the roof.

— All right. I spy, with my little eye, something beginning with M, giggles Monkey.

— MONKEY, I say.

— Uh-uh, says Monkey.

— ME, I say.

— Uh-uh, says Monkey.

— I give up, I say.

Monkey turns round and bends over and looks at me from between his legs and says, MY BUTT!

And then we both laugh and laugh and laugh til we cry which is a Pink feeling and I try not to look at where he had the TERRIBLE INJURY which is a big hole above his bum where his tail should be because that might take away the Pink and I want it to last forever.

But then Monkey suddenly stops laughing and he starts going ooh ooh ah ah.

And I say, What's wrong, Monkey?

And he says, It's my injuries, man. My injuries.

And I say, Let me help you. Then I carefully PUSH the stuffing back into his BUM because some of it's slipped out, what with all the bending over and laughing.

This kind of thing happens to Monkey a lot since the TERRIBLE DAY when he got hit by a car and his tail got RIPPED OFF. He can be happy as anything, but then he remembers the accident or he gets BAD PAIN and it makes him sad.

I wish I'd been there to protect him but I wasn't, which makes me feel Turquoise GUILTY. So now I never let him go anywhere without me because I want to keep him safe.

He says, Ahhhh. That's better. Wow! I love you, man.

And I kiss his hand and say, I love you too, Monkey.

And he says, Hey, you know how I know we're best buddies?

And I say, No. How?

And he says, Because only a best buddy would push stuffin' back into his best buddy's tush.

And that makes us laugh again, but this time I hold my hand over the HOLE in his bottom so that the stuffing does NOT spill out again because BEST FRIENDS do this kind of thing too.

Megan

There's a glow of light and muffled laughter seeping out from under Dad's coat. I can't help but smile. It's nice to hear Daniel laughing at least. We used to make each other crack up all the time.

I just wish it was *me* making him laugh like that right now.

Mum dumps a stack of thick textbooks onto the doctor's desk. Multicoloured Post-it notes stick out from between their pages. She riffles through one of the books, her hands jerky and twitchy, till she finds the page she's looking for.

'Here,' she says, planting a finger in a highlighted sentence and shoving the book towards the doctor. 'This sounds a lot like Daniel's condition.'

The doctor scans it and nods. 'Yes. Certainly there are some similarities, although . . .'

Mum thrusts another two books at her. 'And this one. This could be it. Or this one here.'

The doctor doesn't read the books this time. 'Well. You've clearly done your research.'

'She hasn't been sleeping,' says Dad.

Mum angrily slams one of the books shut. 'Course I haven't. I work all day. And somebody's got to find out what's up with him. My gorgeous boy is ...' Her voice cracks. 'And nobody can tell us anything.'

She squeezes her lips together to stop herself crying. This happens a lot.

Dad puts his hand on her shoulder. 'Come on, Karen. He's doing great. He just needs love and time.'

Mum brushes him off. 'It's been six weeks, Jim. Open your eyes.' She turns to the doctor and waves a hand at Dad. 'You see what I'm up against? He doesn't think there's a problem.'

Dad shakes his head. 'Daniel *is* getting better. I was playing football with him just this morning.'

The doctor raises her eyebrows.

'No, you weren't,' says Mum. 'I was watching. You were kicking the ball against him and it was bouncing off.'

'He scored a brilliant header past me.'

'Only when you booted it at his face.'

Dad sinks into his chair, sulking like a little boy.

'So I understand you're a deputy head teacher, Mrs Chadwick,' says the doctor to Mum. 'You must have to work long hours.'

'Yes,' says Mum, rubbing her eyes. 'Not that I'm doing a very good job at the moment.'

'And Mr Chadwick. You are ...'

'I'm a sculptor,' says Dad. 'I make big model animals out of scrap metal.'

The doctor nods. She looks impressed.

'But mainly I'm a stay-at-home dad. Before the accident, Daniel found school hard sometimes. Whenever things got a bit much, the school let me teach him at home.'

'Teach him!' snorts Mum. 'Mainly they just chuffed about all day in their pants, watching *Star Wars* or playing with Lego or something.'

Dad shifts uneasily. 'It wasn't *always* like that.'

Er . . . yes, it was.

The doctor nods.

Dad seems to take this as another criticism. 'Daniel *needs* time out,' he says, a bit loudly. 'Too much school isn't good for him. And you don't have to be sitting at a desk to be learning.'

Mum purses her lips.

'*O-kay,*' says the doctor, trying to move on. 'I understand that Daniel was run over outside a . . . fish and chip shop.'

'He wanted to get the food into the car,' says Dad. 'He was over-excited.'

'Can't think whose fault that was,' says Mum to the ceiling.

Dad smiles weakly. 'We were visiting all the chip shops in Preston, see. One every week. Daniel needed to find the best one. It was really important to him. To all of us.'

He's right. Fish and chips are *really* important in our house. We've never been able to go out for dinner like other families, not with Daniel being the way he is. Plus he only ever eats orange and yellow food. So fish and chips in the kitchen is the closest we ever get to having a proper meal out.

If the doctor had asked me, of course I could've remembered every single detail about the whole evening for her.

But like I said, nobody cares what I think.

HALF AN HOUR
BEFORE THE ACCIDENT

Megan

'Do you *need* the hat and magnifying glass, Snotface?' I say to Daniel.

We're in the hallway, waiting for Dad to come in from his work shed so we can go to the chippy. He's always late.

'Yes, I ACTUALLY do,' says Daniel. The hat's one of those Sherlock Holmes ones with the flaps. His eye goes massive as he peers at me through the magnifying glass. 'Daddy says they're important tools for finding CLUES and EVIDENCE.'

Daniel's voice is flat like a robot's, but he emphasises some words really loudly.

'At least leave the pipe here,' I say.

'All detectives smoke pipes, and that's a SCIENTIFIC FACT,' he says.

Then he holds up Monkey to his ear and makes a *wussawussa* noise.

'EXCELLENT PLAN, Monkey,' he says. 'We CAN suck our chips up through the pipe. Or even SMOKE them.'

Jeez. The kid's off his nut.

Mum comes bustling into the house and goes straight to the walk-in cupboard by the front door. 'Sorry I'm late. Meeting with a parent. How was your day, Megan?' she calls out to me.

It's hard not to smile, even though I'm blushing. 'Really good. I got ninety-six per cent in my history test, and my new piano teacher reckons I'm ready for Grade Five.'

'Clever girl!' says Mum from the cupboard. 'That's wonderful.'

I find myself blushing.

'Megan's a MEGA NERD and she's got a library up her BUM!' says Daniel.

I pretend to be mad at him and give him a rib tickle. I'm not a nerd anyway. I just work hard, that's all.

'Not nice, Daniel,' says Mum. 'And how are you?'

'Great!' says Daniel. 'Daddy and me made a ROBOT out of CHOCOLATE MOUSSE POTS but first we had to eat SIX chocolate mousses EACH.'

'Oh.' Inside the cupboard, I can hear her taking off her work shoes and putting them away. 'I thought you were meant to be in school today.'

'I came home for LUNCH and Daddy gave me the AFTERNOON off.'

'Did he now?' says Mum.

'Yes. MrsMaryWoodcock said I was OKAY, but Daddy

thought I looked PALE and STRESSED OUT.'

Dad always says school stresses Daniel out. This is sort of true, but sometimes I think Dad keeps Daniel at home because he wants to eat six chocolate mousses instead of doing work.

Mum comes out of the cupboard. She gives us both a hug. Then she has a second look at Daniel, narrowing her eyes. 'Why are you dressed like that, Daniel?'

'For collecting CLUES and EVIDENCE, Mummy, because Friday night is CHIP SHOP CHALLENGE NIGHT. Don't you know ANYTHING?'

'Of course,' says Mum tightly.

Just then I hear Dad coming in the back door. 'Hey, Big D. I've sprayed it silver and . . .'

He comes into the hall in his overalls, holding a silver model robot in his hands. He notices Mum. 'Oh, hello.'

'Hard at work then,' says Mum, folding her arms.

'Well, I'd finished that big giraffe for the zoo in France, and I thought Daniel needed a break.'

Mum blows her hair out of her eyes. 'All right for some.'

'Anyway,' says Dad, clapping his hands together, 'who's ready for Chip Shop Challenge Night?'

Daniel and I both cheer.

Dad poses with his arms out and speaks in that gruff American accent they use on film adverts. 'One family's quest to find the perfect chip shop. Starring: the Chadwicks as . . . themselves. And. Some dead fish and sliced potatoes . . . also as . . . themselves.'

Mum pretends to look exasperated. Dad's jokes are super-lame, but he's one of those people who just makes you laugh no matter what they say.

He bends Mum backwards and gives her a kiss on the lips.

Urgh.

'Ah, ma cherie,' he says, switching to an awful French accent. 'I must whisk you away to la restaurant of your dreams – the 'Eavenly Cod.'

'Oh wow. You *really* know how to treat a lady,' says Mum, straightening up and slipping on some trainers. 'Ah well – I suppose we need something to replace the Happy Haddock.'

A few months ago, our local chippy – the Happy Haddock – suddenly closed down. We'd gone there every Friday and family celebration since time began. Then, one night when we turned up, the lights were off and there was a sign in the window: 'CLOSED PERMANENTLY DUE TO FAMILY ISSUES. SORRY FOR THE INCONVENIENCE.'

The inconvenience?

As far as Daniel was concerned, they might as well have closed down the earth or switched off the sun.

That night he had the biggest nuclear meltdown ever – punching holes in doors, headbutting walls, the lot. It took

Dad three hours to calm him down, and he had to promise Daniel that we'd go to every chippy in the city till we found one that was even better.

'Can we just GO NOW?' says Daniel.

'How many have we been to so far, Snotface? Ten?' I ask, trying to distract him. I can see he's getting cross – the Red mood, he calls it.

'Thirteen, ACTUALLY,' says Daniel. He pulls his red notebook out of his duffel-coat pocket. The notebook has 'CHIP SHOP CHALLENGE LOGBOOK. TOP SECRET – AUTHORISED PERSONNEL ONLY' on the front.

He uses Monkey's paw to turn the pages of it. 'Week one: East End Fish Bar. It was NICE but Mummy got that shrivelled-up GREEN CHIP that Daddy said looked like a little willy with a NASTY DISEASE. EIGHT OUT OF TEN. Week two: Ali's Fish 'n' Chips 'n' Kebabs. I did NOT like the way the sweaty kebab SPUN ROUND so I felt all Purple and I was sick on that man's shoes an—'

'All right. We get it,' I say, clamping my hand over his mouth. Daniel makes this dramatic *mphmphmph* noise until we both double up laughing. Then Dad whips off his overalls and we walk to the car.

'How many more have we got to visit?' asks Mum.

'Eleven,' says Daniel. 'Then we'll know which is NUMERO UNO in the whole city.'

'Oh, that's –'

'BUT,' he continues, 'Daddy says that THEN we'll find the best one in BRITAIN.'

'Really?' says Mum, giving Dad a *when were you going to tell me about that?* look over the top of the car.

Dad gulps. He's always coming up with crazy ideas. But if you make Daniel a promise – no matter how stupid – he'll remember it forever. And trust me, you don't want to let him down.

'I thought it might be fun.'

We get in the car.

'Daddy cut out a LIST of the BEST FIVE from a magazine and stuck it in HERE,' says Daniel, waving his notebook over the back of Mum's seat. 'We only have to visit these FIVE, because we know that all the other chip shops in the whole country are WORSE.'

'That's a relief,' says Mum, huffing out her cheeks.

'And you'll never guess,' says Dad, suddenly excited. 'Totally random. The number-one chip shop in Britain is the one wh—'

Mum raises a hand to interrupt him. 'Let's talk about it later. We'll have to pick Grandma up on the way. She's staying here for the weekend.'

'Excellent,' says Daniel. 'After tea I can play her at Connect Four. I am currently winning three hundred and forty-five games to two because she is RUBBISH!'

Megan

The doctor comes over to the corner where Daniel and I are sitting.

'And how are **you** getting on?' she asks me.

Surprised to be spoken to, I feel redness building up on my neck. What I want to say is: *Terrible. I can't face school any more, so I'm doing really badly when I used to be top of the class for everything. I can't even be bothered to practise the piano. I'm upset all the time. I feel like I've lost my brother. Mum and Dad are so busy arguing that they hardly notice me. The whole time it's like there's a massive hot-air balloon in the back of my throat, and I just want my family back.*

But I don't say this. I don't really say very much at all these days.

Instead I just shrug and hide behind my hair.

'It's hard, I know,' says the doctor kindly, but then she turns her back on me, crouching down so she can ease Dad's woolly coat up over Daniel's head. 'Hello, Daniel. Are you comfortable under there?'

Daniel gazes back with those gorgeous-but-empty brown eyes. The torch has dropped to the floor. He's holding Monkey up next to his face, like it's also looking at her. The effect is quite creepy.

'Your monkey's lost his tail,' she says.

Daniel says nothing, doesn't even blink.

'It got ripped off in the accident,' says Mum.

Dad scratches his neck. 'Then we kind of *lost* it.'

'I see,' says the doctor. Still holding up the edge of Dad's coat, she twists her head round to face Mum and Dad. 'Have you seen any improvements? Has he recognised you? Spoken to you at all?'

'Well,' says Dad, 'this morning I asked him if he wanted fish and chips for breakfast – family joke, see – and he *definitely* grunted at me.'

'He was grunting at Monkey,' says Mum flatly. 'Like always.'

'Hmmm,' says the doctor. 'So he's still attached to the toy monkey?'

'It was his fiddle toy before the accident,' says Dad. 'He's always taken it everywhere with him, since he was tiny. Gives his fingers something to do. Sometimes he sucks its hand or flicks its legs to keep himself calm.'

'But since the accident it's more like he's . . . I don't know . . .' says Mum.

'Friends with it?' offers the doctor.

'Obsessed with it, more like,' says Mum. 'Talks to it all the time. Hides behind it.'

'Have you tried removing it from him?' asks the doctor.

'Once. We tried to wash it after the accident,' says Dad. 'It didn't go well.'

In fact, it went *really badly*. Daniel kicked Dad in the face and gave him a nosebleed.

'Well, I can't be sure . . .' says the doctor, 'but I wonder if the toy monkey acts as a barrier, a shield, from the world. He's had a big shock and somehow the cuddly toy protects him from further pain.'

I feel like saying, *Duh! Do you think so?*

I tried to tell Mum and Dad exactly this a month ago. They weren't really listening to me.

The doctor turns back to Daniel and reaches forward. 'Hi, Daniel. I wonder if I could shake your monkey's hand? I'd really like to get to know him.'

I say, 'I wouldn't do th—'

But it's too late.

The change is sudden and violent, like a firework going off. Daniel throws himself on to his tummy, clutching Monkey under him. He starts kicking and punching the floor and screaming.

The doctor doesn't seem all that surprised by this. 'OK. OK. I'm sorry, Daniel. I'm moving away now.'

She stands. Straight away, Daniel jolts up again and yanks the coat back over his head.

Daniel and Monkey

— It's OK, I say to Monkey because he had a WIG-OUT, which happens sometimes on account of his TERRIBLE ACCIDENT and it's my job to calm him down because I'm officially his BEST FRIEND.

— Did you hear what that woman said? he says.

— No, I say.

There are other people in the room. That's why we're hiding in our SPECIAL SECRET HIDEOUT. I don't know who the people are and I don't recognise them but Monkey says PEOPLE ARE BAD, so we NEED to stay away from them.

One of the people spoke to me but I couldn't understand her. Her voice was just noise, like WAARK WAARK WAARK. Monkey can understand other people though, so sometimes he tells me what they say.

— They wanna to split us up, man. They wanna take me away from you, he says.

— No! I won't LET them! I say, and I feel very Orange but also Red and Grey and the moods are swirling round each other and I don't like it.

— I can't be without you, buddy, I just can't, says

25

Monkey, and he is crying. He often cries since he got HIT BY A CAR and LOST HIS TAIL.

— You never will be, I say.

— Thanks D-Dog. You're the greatest.

Then I say, Let's get outta here.

And I put on an American voice for this, which is what I sometimes do to cheer Monkey up.

Monkey says, Just us?

— Course, I say.

And he says, How 'bout out on the ocean? You, me and the fishes, and nobody else to ruin it, right?

— Right! I say, and we come out of the secret hideout and it turns out that all along we've been sitting on a TINY PATCH OF SAND that pops out from the sea like a turtle's shell, and we're surrounded by beautiful water, blue and glittery as far as I can see, and a little ROWING BOAT is bobbing up and down with 'D-Dog and Monkey' painted on the side, and Monkey and me climb into it facing each other and Monkey starts to row and off we float across the calm sea, and I smile big and wide with the Pink feeling and I DON'T look at the big horrible sea monsters as we glide past them.

Megan

So it's all got a bit strange.

The doctor has sat back down at the desk, trying not to look flustered. Meanwhile, Daniel's shuffling round the room in a totally different world. He's holding Monkey in front of his face, turning its wrists in circles and mumbling to himself.

'All right, Snotface?' I say to him half-heartedly as he passes me. He doesn't answer.

'So I understand that Daniel has a diagnosis of autism,' says the doctor, watching him go past.

This is an important thing: Daniel is autistic.

It sort of explains a lot about him, like how powerful his moods are, and how he sees the world differently to everyone else. It sometimes makes his life – and everyone else's – really difficult. I try not to make too much of a big deal out of it though. It's just a part of who he is. Without it, he wouldn't be Daniel.

'And?' says Dad.

'Being run over was a massive shock to Daniel,' says the doctor. 'And autistic people can be particularly sensitive to these shocks.'

'And?' says Dad again. He never seems to trust anyone

who tries to tell him anything about Daniel.

'Well. You say that, along with everything else, he doesn't seem to recognise you,' says the doctor.

'Not since the accident, no,' says Mum.

'You don't know that for sure,' Dad says huffily. It's hard for him to accept that he and Daniel aren't best buddies any more.

'Perhaps he's developed some form of face blindness?' offers the doctor.

'He's blind?' exclaims Dad.

'No,' says the doctor, holding her hands up. 'Sometimes autistic people can't recognise faces.'

'So what does he see? Blank skin? Strangers?' I find myself saying.

Amazingly, the doctor answers me. 'Perhaps. Perhaps it's blurry. Perhaps he doesn't even realise he's not seeing you properly – like a gap in his vision he doesn't even know about.'

'You said he wasn't brain-damaged,' says Dad.

'Correct,' says the doctor. 'All the scans show that his brain's working fine. So what's causing it?'

'We were hoping you'd tell us,' says Mum.

The doctor tilts her head. 'Maybe Daniel's seeing and hearing things but his brain doesn't understand them. Or maybe – and this is what I suspect – his brain is somehow *choosing* what it *wants* to understand.'

'I think I've read about this,' says Mum. 'Selective processing, or something?'

'Sounds far-fetched,' says Dad.

'Brains are complicated,' says the doctor, shrugging. 'Autistic people often don't like surprises. And the accident was a huge surprise that turned Daniel's life upside down. Who knows? Maybe part of his brain doesn't trust the world any more.'

'He trusts *us*,' snaps Dad.

'Now it's not really my area of expertise . . .' says the doctor, trying to ignore him. 'But good news – there's a specialist research centre that's just opened. I emailed them and they'd love to work with Daniel. If you agree, of course.'

'Perfect!' says Mum. 'When can he go?'

'Whoa whoa whoa,' says Dad. 'Research? You mean testing things out on him? Like he's a . . . a rat in a cage. I don't like it.'

'These are some of the world's top experts,' says the doctor soothingly. 'They'd be *very* sensitive to Daniel's needs. Everything would be geared towards him – his treatments, his food, the room where he'd be staying.'

'But he's never had a night away from home before,' says Dad uneasily. 'Where is this *research centre*?'

'Cambridge.'

'*Cambridge?!*' shrieks Dad. 'That's two hundred miles

away! What about his family? He needs to be here. With people who love him.'

'One of us could stay down there with him,' says Mum.

'What? And split the family apart? No,' says Dad.

I feel like I'm being pulled in two. I want Daniel to be better. I *need* him to be better. But I couldn't be two hundred miles from him. It'd break my heart.

'I understand that this is a big decision . . .' begins the doctor.

But Dad's already on his feet. 'The answer's no.'

'We need to discuss this,' says Mum angrily.

Dad picks his coat up off the floor and guides Daniel and me towards the exit. Daniel keeps rotating Monkey's arms round and round, as if they're dancing, or rowing a boat or something. 'Any other pearls of wisdom, doctor?' asks Dad as we pass her desk.

The doctor stays calm. 'Try to keep him stimulated. Think about what he can see and smell and touch and –'

Before I know it, we're out of the room and back in the corridor.

'Hey!' says Mum, following us out. 'What are you doing? This clinic might be exactly what he needs.'

'I can think of two hundred reasons why it isn't,' says Dad, his hand laid gently on Daniel's back as he guides him away along the corridor.

TEN MINUTES
BEFORE DANIEL'S ACCIDENT

Megan

The smell of fish and chips grabs us as soon as we step out of the car.

It's the smell of family.

Immediately it takes you home: Dad dumping fistfuls of them out onto warm plates; scrunched-up, greasy paper spread across the worktops; steamy windows; everyone swarming around trying to pinch a stray chip. Chattering voices:

Let me put them out before you start mauling them.

You shouldn't have got large – we'll never be able to eat them all.

Which ones have got no salt on?

I swear I ordered another fish.

Don't tell me we've run out of ketchup.

Hey! He's got more than me!

Noisy. Crazy. Warm. Chaotic. It's what our family's all about.

My mouth's watering and there's a fuzzy feeling in my belly.

We wait for a line of cars to whizz past us before crossing the road. I hold Daniel's hand tightly – he has a habit of rushing into things.

When we get to the front door, Dad taps at the sticker on the glass. 'Five-star hygiene rating,' he says, winking at Daniel. 'Shows they don't wipe their bums on the fish.'

Mum shakes her head but smiles.

Daniel and Monkey look at the sticker through his magnifying glass. Then he jots something in his notebook.

'Karen! I say, Karen!' cries Grandma from across the road. She's leaning out of the car window.

'Are you OK?' says Mum.

Grandma has to pull her neck in as a lorry roars past. Dad parked on the double yellows with her Blue Badge on the dashboard, as if that makes it OK.

'Can you see if they've got any baked beans, Karen?' calls Grandma, when the lorry's gone. 'I've been struggling to go to the *lavatory* for the last few days.'

What a lovely thought.

She tries to make out like she's whispering, but actually she says it louder than most people can shout.

'Got you,' says Mum.

'A nice tub of beans should ease things along!' Grandma continues.

'All right. We get the picture,' I say, looking over my shoulder to make sure nobody else can hear her. Sometimes my family is so embarrassing.

'Have you not got a couple of tins in your bumbag?' says Dad.

I laugh. This is one of our family jokes. Grandma wears a bumbag ALL THE TIME. It's massive – like the size of a shoe box – and she's very secretive about what's inside. She has a little padlock for it and wears the key round her neck. Dad always makes fun of her for what she might keep in there – an elephant, her broomstick, the bodies of her victims.

Three more cars whizz past.

'It's a busy road,' says Mum. 'Are you sure Grandma'll be all right in the car?'

'Course,' says Dad. 'She's as tough as a hedgehog's hairbrush.'

The moment we open the chip shop door we're hit by a wall of warm, tangy, vinegary goodness. There's a queue, which is always a brilliant sign. A loud sizzling sound comes from behind the counter as a basket of chips is dropped into the fat.

'Ahhhhh! Fish and chips!' says Dad, taking a deep breath. 'You know, if it wasn't for fish and chips . . .'

'We'd never have been born!' say Daniel and I together, finishing off the sentence before he can.

Dad pretends to look surprised and hurt. 'Oh. Have you heard the story before?'

'Only about a million times,' I say.

'Tell it again! Tell it again!' cries Daniel, waving Monkey about.

'Well,' says Dad, 'your mum and I were both students at art college in London, see. It was midnight and I was at the chip van, grabbing some late supper. And then your mother comes over to me. Did you know, she was a punk in those days? Purple hair, nose ring, clumpy boots, sass.'

'Were you, Mummy? Were you?' asks Daniel, even though he's seen the photos. It *is* hard to picture her like that now though, with her sensible short brown hair and teacher-clothes.

Mum tuts. 'I was a silly girl.'

'Anyway –' Dad grins – 'so she came over, and she stole a chip, and then she –'

'Stole your heart. We know,' I say in my boredest voice, even though deep down I love the story.

And Dad kisses Mum on the lips, and I put my fingers down my throat and pretend to puke, and Daniel says, '*Yuck!*' and covers Monkey's eyes so it doesn't have to watch.

Dad bends down to Daniel and whispers, 'Hey, don't take the hygiene sticker's word for it, Big D. Have a snoop about. There might be dirty nappies under the battered sausages or an old pigeon being sick into the gravy.'

Daniel gets Monkey to salute. Then he drops to his tummy and crawls off along the floor. I can tell he's getting excited, examining every tile, every nook and cranny.

'Really?' says Mum.

'He's fine,' says Dad.

We keep moving forward till we're second in the queue.

'How long will the chips be?' the woman in front of us asks the man serving.

Dad leans forward, holding out his finger and thumb. 'About three or four centimetres, I reckon.'

He gets a laugh from the man behind the counter, and the woman in the queue says he's a real card, whatever that means. But I've heard the joke ten times before.

'That is a GOOD JOKE!' Daniel says from the floor. 'Because long can be TIME or actually LENGTH.'

His voice is loud and fast and he's furiously sucking on Monkey's hand. He's very excited now – he calls this the Blue mood.

'Shhh, Snotface,' I say to him. It doesn't take much for him to go over the top. Ignoring me, he wriggles away across the floor like a caterpillar.

Just then, Grandma comes barrelling into the shop, her walking stick clunking on the tiles and her bumbag bouncing with each step. 'Not been served yet? I could've grown the potatoes myself by now.'

'I thought you were waiting in the car,' says Dad.

'The way those drivers go shooting past? No, thank you. Gives me the collywobbles. And I've changed my mind about the baked beans. I'll have mushy peas instead. They'll grease the wheels all right.'

I feel sick. Why are old people so grim?

'Grandma needs a POO!' cries Daniel, leaping to his feet.

A few people behind us snigger. Grandma goes red.

'Calm down,' says Mum, but you can tell she finds it funny.

Daniel snaps his notebook shut. 'The hygiene inspection is COMPLETE!' he announces. Then he drops his voice to a loud whisper. 'I don't think they wipe their bums on the fish.'

Dad and I crack up laughing. Mum snorts. Even Grandma forgets her embarrassment and has a little chuckle.

Fish. Chips. Family. Laughter. It doesn't get much better than this, right?

Daniel and Monkey

Monkey and me have been rowing our boat for ages. Then the sun comes out and Monkey says, Yo, D-Dog. Let's be pirates.

This is an EXCELLENT IDEA. So I close one eye and say in my bestest ever pirate voice, Aaaarrgh, me hearty. Me name is Captain Bumbeard O'Trumpleton and I'm a cut-throat buccaneer.

And Monkey tucks his leg up under his bottom and says, Ahoy there, matey. I'm Peg Leg McWillywhistle. Haul the Jolly Roger and let's be a sailin'.

– Aye aye, Peg Leg. We's got scurvy dogs to run through an' booty to plunder.

– Aaaaarrrr!

– Aaaaarrrr!

And his pirate voice is better than mine, but he doesn't make a big deal about it because best friends DON'T do that sort of thing.

Megan

So now we're walking down this endless glass hospital corridor, not talking to each other. The autumn sunlight coming through the big windows is warm and our feet squeak on the lino.

Three words keep flying round my brain: *two hundred miles*.

I get it – he needs help. He needs *something*. But it's just too far away. Way too far. He'd have to stay away. And so would Dad, probably. And who knows how long they'd be there for?

Daniel's walking alongside me. Monkey's sitting on his shoulder, and Daniel's making all these loud, throaty *aaaaarrrghhh* noises. He's got one eye closed and he's holding one of Monkey's legs back under its bottom. Up ahead, I can see a pink balloon bouncing about above the heads of the people walking towards us. *Congratulations! Baby girl!* It's such a happy message that I feel a horrible knot growing in my belly.

The corridor's busy so I can't see who's holding it. But then there's a break in the stream of people and I recognise a familiar woman waddling towards us.

'Hey!' I say. 'Isn't that MrsMaryWoodcock?'

MrsMaryWoodcock is Daniel's teaching assistant from school. You have to say her name like that – all one word – because that's how Daniel says it.

When she first started with him in Foundation Stage, he was wild – attacking people, shrieking, shoving sticks into his eyes. But over the years she's slowly helped him to get more comfortable and settled at school.

By the time of his accident, he could read a bit, write a bit and stay in class for some of the time. Believe me, for Daniel, this was a massive deal.

Even Dad likes her, and he hates pretty much everything to do with Daniel going to school.

It was MrsMaryWoodcock who came up with the idea of giving his moods different colours: Pink for happy, Red for angry, Grey for sad, Blue for over-excited. There are other ones too. I've never figured out if he actually sees the colours or not, but it's always seemed to help him. At school he had a set of cards he could hold up to show people how he was feeling.

I'm so pleased she's here. If anyone can help him now, it's her.

THE ACCIDENT

Megan

In the chip shop, everybody's laughter dies down. Apart from Daniel's, that is. He keeps going for at least ten seconds longer than everyone else – *ha-ha-ha-ha* like a machine gun. I squint at him. As well as being excited, he's getting really silly now, waggling his head and waving Monkey like mad. Green and Blue at the same time. Not a good combination. It's always possible though – one big mood can easily get mixed up with another. I put my hand on his shoulder but he shrugs me off and bounces away around the shop, pulling the elastic waistband of his trousers out.

'Look at me, Daddy! I'm a kangaroo! Boing! Boing! Put the chips in my pouch!'

Mum apologises to the man behind the counter as Dad orders the food.

Daniel blows a raspberry and starts playing bongos on the metal counter with Monkey's hands, sending grains of salt bouncing up into the air. 'How much *LONGER?!*' he groans, stamping his feet. 'This is taking *AGES!*'

'Easy, Big D,' says Dad.

'Going as fast as I can,' says the man, wrapping the first tray and popping it into an open carrier bag on the counter.

Daniel's twitching now, licking his lips in the way that always makes them red and sore. He sucks on Monkey's hand, then spits it out again.

'I CAN'T WAIT ANY MORE!' he announces. Then he *lunges* forward, rips the corner off the paper and shoves a couple of chips into his mouth. 'Oooh ah ah.'

'Was that you or Monkey?' I joke, but it's too late for that.

'So good. So good,' he pants. 'Got to get them back into the car because the COOL BAG is in there and it keeps things WARM and not just COLD because you have to eat chips HOT and the plates haven't been WARMED because Mummy is here and not at home because of Grandma who can't go to the bog.'

His little body can't cope with the power of his mood when he's like this. It's like shaking up a can of Coke then opening it. The chip shop man looks at him funnily as he puts the final tray into the bag.

'AT LAST!' says Daniel. And before we can stop him, he's grabbed the bag of food and darted out into the street and I'm after him and I tell him to wait but he's all confused, running this way – that way – this way –

that way and pushing the fingers of his free hand into his eyeballs and I go to pull him back, but he slips through my grasp and runs into the road.

There's a *screech*. A *crunch*. A horrible wet *thud*.

Megan

We squeak our way along the corridor towards MrsMaryWoodcock. She's small and round and old – maybe seventy – and her smile is like a warm hug.

'Hiya, Daniel,' she says. She has a gentle, sing-song Liverpudlian accent. 'What a lovely surprise. Feeling better?'

Daniel just stares right through her.

'I've missed you at school,' MrsMaryWoodcock says. She jiggles the pink balloon up and down. There's a bunch of flowers in her other hand. 'I'm just visiting me new granddaughter. She's lovely.'

'Look who it is, Daniel,' says Dad.

Still nothing.

MrsMaryWoodcock turns to Dad. 'I was just thinking about him the other day, y'know. When he got that certificate in assembly last year. Oh, I was dead proud. D'you remember, Daniel?'

Not a flicker.

I remember. The certificate's still on the fridge: 'For spending five whole mornings in class this week and for writing a lovely story.'

It doesn't sound like much (and yes, the story was rubbish – *Once there was a monkey called Monkey who ate some chips. The End)* but trust me – for Daniel this was amazing.

I was still at primary school then. He went up to collect it in assembly, getting Monkey to take it off Miss Bassett with its soggy hands. I got so choked up that I ran up to him in front of the whole school and gave him a massive hug and told him how much I love him and everyone started clapping and MrsMaryWoodcock had tears in her eyes.

'Shame,' she says to herself.

There's something unbelievably sad about this. Daniel LOVES MrsMaryWoodcock. I feel my throat tightening up.

Then something amazing happens.

Daniel focuses on MrsMaryWoodcock. He's still got one eye closed and his other eye narrows a little bit in concentration. 'Tiffcat,' he grunts, finally.

And we all freeze.

Oh. My. God.

He spoke.

He spoke.

Actual words.

Tiffcat. *Certificate.* We're all gawping at him open-mouthed. I go to hug him but then I step back. There's something unsettling about the look on his face.

Dad's too excited to notice this though. 'See!' he says, squeezing Daniel's shoulder and jabbing a finger towards Mum. 'See! He doesn't need some stupid clinic a million miles away. He'll get better with us. Ha ha! Nice one, Danny lad! Perfect timing! I knew you could do it!'

Daniel looks at each of us in turn. Then he slowly turns back to face MrsMaryWoodcock and lifts Monkey off his shoulder.

Daniel and Monkey

So we were rowing along the ocean looking for Spanish ships to sink and sailors to run through with our cutlasses, which are long swords all curvy like deadly bananas. And suddenly we almost got RAMMED into by this boat and it had a woman's head at the front of it carved out of wood and I recognised the face of the woman but I didn't know why, and then something weird happened because the face started SPEAKING and it said tiffcat and I copied it because I thought it was really strange and then Monkey shouted, IGNORE HER!

And then he went totally cracker-mad-mental all of a sudden and he jumped on the boat COMPLETELY WILD and started wrecking it, RIPPING up the sails and SMASHING the masts with his monkey fists and I tried to stop him but he ROARED at me. You don't know nothing! You ain't had to lose your tail, man!

And I felt deepest Orange, which means VERY SCARED.

Megan

The car is silent but the silence isn't empty – it's solid and dangerous and lashing about the tight space, like one of those metal spiky balls that medieval soldiers used to swing. I'm still trembling from what happened in the corridor.

It was so awful, and it happened so quickly we couldn't do anything about it.

With no warning, Daniel just started absolutely whacking MrsMaryWoodcock with his fists and with Monkey. She was squealing and holding up her pudgy little hands to defend herself but he was too fast for her. We eventually dragged him off her, his teeth bared and his eyes wide.

Dad scooped him up and carried him away, with Mum apologising desperately over her shoulder as she followed, rubbing Daniel's hand to try and settle him down. But Daniel was already settled again, like someone had pushed a switch to turn off the Red.

MrsMaryWoodcock stared after us, the balloon bobbing uselessly against the ceiling, the flowers crushed and battered in her hand and her broken glasses lying on the floor.

Dad starts the car and eases out of the car park.

Then, very softly, Mum says, 'I think he needs to go to that clinic.'

'No,' snaps Dad. 'We're not talking about it.'

'B—'

'No!'

I feel my stomach tensing up. He never used to get angry like this.

I glance over at Daniel. He's quietly cuddling Monkey and making all these calming, clucking noises, like he's holding a baby.

I wish I could see inside his head.

Daniel and Monkey

Monkey is crying.

— I'm sorry, man, he says.

— That's OK. Everyone gets mad sometimes, I say, and I stroke his head because this is a nice way to calm someone down who's upset.

— I guess I heard you talking to . . . you know . . .

— The boat.

Monkey raises one eyebrow which is a CONFUSED expression. Then he says, Yeah, man. The boat. That's right. You were talking to **the boat**. Of course. Anyways, I just got scared. I got the Orange real bad, then I got the Red.

— But why?

— Can't you see it, man? People are trying to take you away from me.

— I'll never let them! I say.

— Then you start talking to that . . . boat. I get spooked — like what if you leave me? I can't live without you, man. I can't.

Then Monkey bursts into terrible tears. I hug him really, really tightly and I say, But I'll never leave you, Monkey. I LOVE you.

Then Monkey is snivelling and snot is dripping everywhere and he says, I ain't the same monkey I was before the accident, man. How can I be a monkey without no tail?

I want to tell him about barbary macaques which are monkeys which only have small tails in their bums that you can't really see. But someone told me once that you shouldn't try to teach upset people facts even if those facts are SUPER-

INTERESTING, because maybe they're not in the mood to learn and you might make things worse.

– It must be horrible, I say instead, because agreeing with a sad person is a good way to SOOTHE them.

– I ain't nothing without you, big guy.

– I'll look after you, Monkey. I promise. You're my best pal and we'll be TOGETHER FOREVER.

I squeeze Monkey SUPER-TIGHT but I feel strange. What ARE barbary macaques? And where have I seen the face on the front of that boat before?

Megan

We come into the house. As usual, Grandma's in her chair in the front room, watching some antiques programme on telly. Her feet are up on the pouffe and her bumbag sits on her skinny belly like a mountain.

'Karen. I say, Karen –' she says as we walk in.

'Not now,' replies Mum, taking off her shoes.

Daniel clomps upstairs. Dad storms off to the kitchen.

Grandma carries on talking at Mum. 'Did you wash this bra?'

This is typical Grandma. After the accident, she moved in so she could 'help us out', but she just causes more work for everybody, and she doesn't seem to notice anybody else's feelings.

Grandma pulls down her top to reveal her wrinkly chest, which is completely gross. I turn away. 'Because there's a stain on it, Karen. I think it's soup. I can't go round with a dirty bra on.'

'Nobody's going to see it,' says Mum, angrily shoving the books from her bag back onto the bookcase.

'*I'll* see it. And anyway, you never know, I might die this afternoon . . .'

Not this again.

'Fancy dying in a dirty bra,' she goes on. 'What would people think? I'm going to take it off now, Karen.'

Mum marches off out of the room.

Grandma sits there, open-mouthed. 'I wonder what's got into her,' she says. 'It's only a bra.'

I don't know how to answer that.

'Ooh, do us a cup of tea, Megan,' she says to me. 'And make it stronger this time. That one you made this morning was weaker than a spider's urine sample.'

'Later, Grandma,' I say. 'I'm going to check on Daniel.'

'I'll die of thirst at this rate,' she calls after me as I run upstairs.

When I go into his room, I don't even bother saying, *All*

right, Snotface, to him. He's lying inside the little wooden playhouse Dad built for him a few years ago, his legs poking out through the curtained doorway. It was always his place to go when things were getting too much. As usual, I can hear him muttering away at Monkey.

Hardly anything's been moved since he got run over: the endless, scattered pictures and papier mâché models he used to make with Dad of volcanoes and dinosaurs and planets and whatever else he was obsessed with for that particular five minutes of his life. The Lego city he built over last summer that takes up half the floor, with every detail you could possibly imagine. (*But Daddy, we NEED a laundrette and a public toilet because they don't have WASHING MACHINES or BOGS in their houses!*) The ring binder where he stored all the maps and plans of our days out. The hole he punched in the door when the Happy Haddock closed.

Sometimes I blame myself for the accident. It's impossible not to. *If only I'd held him tighter. If only I'd rugby-tackled him. If only I'd protected him.* He was just too strong though. Too determined.

I push the thoughts away.

His chip shop notebook is still lying on his desk, where I left it the day after his accident. 'AUTHORISED PERSONNEL ONLY'. I shrug. I guess I count as being authorised.

I pick it up and try to flick through it, but I can't concentrate.

'Why don't you just SPEAK TO US?!' I yell at the little wooden house. I'm surprised by how loud my voice is.

Daniel doesn't even move.

'You're just a . . .' I start but I can't get the words out and I have to get out of here before I start slapping him and now I'm back in my room and I throw myself down on my bed, crying, the notebook still in my hands.

Daniel and Monkey

– What was THAT? I say to Monkey. It sounded like shouting or screaming or something but I couldn't hear any words, just noise. WAARK WAARK WAARK! Again.

Monkey squints like he is looking into the sun or something. And he says, Nothin' for you to worry about, man. Nothin' for you to worry about.

Megan

I've calmed down a bit. I could hear Mum and Dad arguing downstairs but then someone went out, slamming the front door. The house is quiet now, apart from Grandma's loud TV show.

I'm reading Daniel's Chip Shop Challenge Logbook on my bed. It's amazing how much he wrote on each page – more than he'd ever done at school.

I pick pages at random:

'A Kiss on the Chips' Fish and Chip Shop
4/10. The chips were nice and fat but the boy behind the counter had lots of spots and Daddy said watch out because he might squeeze them onto the fish to add extra flavour and I felt Purple even though Daddy said he was joking.

'Robin Spud and Fryer Tuck's Plaice' Fish and Chip Shop
9/10. Chips excellent. Minus one mark because they had a toy fish on the wall and Daddy pressed a button and it sang a song called SITTING ON HAD-DOCK OF THE BAY which Daddy thought was VERY funny but it made me feel like I did NOT want to eat fish so I had Saveloy instead which is a special red

sausage that tastes nice but makes your
burps smelly.

I giggle at the last one but I realise that my cheeks are wet, so I wipe them. I turn the page, which takes me to the last entry he made – the unfinished one from the night of the accident. I don't want to read it, so I close the notebook just as my door opens and Dad walks in.

'Hey,' he says.

It must've been Mum who went out before.

He looks so tired. His eyes are red-rimmed, and his *Star Wars* T-shirt is baggy where he's lost weight.

I want to throw my arms round him, give him a cuddle, but he just hovers at the doorway, sad and confused.

'I heard shouting,' I say.

Dad screws his face up and rubs his eyes. He and Mum have never argued like this before.

'What's going to happen, Dad?'

'I can't let him go away,' he says softly.

'But what if –'

'I just can't!' His voice is firmer. 'We've got to stay together. But your mum . . . I mean, I understand why she . . . but still . . .'

Eventually he notices the notebook in my hand. I hand it to him – something for him to look at, to take his mind off everything, I guess. For a while he turns the pages, occasionally sniffing a sad laugh when he reads something funny that Daniel's written. Then he stops. Stares at one particular page for ages. His brow furrows into a frown as his eyes dance across it, seeming to read it again and again.

Eventually he licks his lips – one of the little mannerisms he shares with Daniel – and closes the notebook. 'Mind if I borrow this?'

He doesn't wait for an answer before dipping out of the room.

He hadn't noticed I was crying.

I'm woken up by Dad throwing open my curtains. 'C'mon. We're going. Everyone else is dressed and ready to rumble.'

I squint at my phone and flop back onto my bed. 'It's quarter past six. Are you trying to kill me?'

I roll over onto my side and pull the covers over my head but Dad whips them off again and dumps them on the floor. 'We've got to take Mum to work.'

'Since when do we do that?' I say, slowly sitting up.

There's a slice of toast and a glass of orange juice on my bedside table. I sit up and take a nibble of the toast. Dad's acting manic, dodging around my room, yanking my uniform out of my cupboard and dropping it onto my chair.

'Hey! Don't touch my pants!' I say, as he pulls open

my underwear drawer. 'It's weird.'

Dad holds up his hands. 'Sure thing. Sorry. Gotta leave in ten though. Your mum's lost her car keys. Terrible shame. And the spare's gone too, would you believe? Where, I don't know. But you see I need the Citroën today, which is a pain, so we're going to have to take her, then drop you off at school after. Got it?'

He's talking crazy-fast, his eyes whizzing about all over the place. He couldn't be more different to yesterday. What on earth's got into him?

I glug some juice. 'But Mum's work is nowhere near my school.'

She works at a big high school in Bolton, which is like twenty miles away. She's always moaning about it. The journey down the motorway can take her an hour if it's busy.

"S why we've gotta go soon. Beat the traffic, see?'

'But I'll be late for sch—'

'Tick tock. Nine minutes now.' Dad grins, before scampering out again.

Everyone's already in the car when I climb in. Mum's in the back, hair wet from the shower, a big bag of marking and her iPad between her feet. She's desperately rooting through her handbag and muttering, 'I *know* I didn't take them out of my bag. This is just what I need. I'm already miles behind on everything.'

Her Fiat 500 is next to us on the drive, windows still covered in condensation.

Up in front, Grandma's moaning that the cold air is bad for her heart, and if this useless oaf ever makes her leave the house at this ungodly hour again she'll knock his bloody teeth out with her walking stick.

It's fair to say that Grandma is *not* a morning person.

Daniel is sitting silently in the middle, Monkey on his lap. Back before the accident, he'd have kicked off massively if we'd changed his routine like this. Every new journey needed to be planned ahead. He'd ask a million questions and demand a full schedule, including pictures. Then he'd insist on following the journey on the map on Dad's phone.

There's something really sad about how he just accepts everything nowadays – docile as a tranquillised cow.

Dad hops in, passes Mum back her reusable coffee cup and rubs his hands together. 'Right then. Off we go.'

He seems cheerful, if a little unhinged.

Grandma seems to notice it too. 'Don't know how you're so lively. I heard you banging about in the night like a flaming grave robber.'

'Yes,' says Mum suspiciously. 'What *were* you doing?'

'Couldn't sleep. Things to do,' says Dad, leering back at her with big wide eyes.

Something very strange is going on here.

He pulls off the driveway.

'Stop!' screams Grandma. Dad slams on the brakes. Mum swears as coffee slops onto her hand. Grandma grabs Dad's wrist. 'My bumbag. I need my bumbag. You rushed me out and I didn't have time to get it.'

'Can we not just get it later?' asks Dad.

'No!' Grandma says. 'Get it now or I'm not coming – not that you've explained to me why I have to come anyway.'

Leaving the car half off the drive, Dad rushes back into the house. He comes back thirty seconds later, pretending to stagger under the weight of the enormous bumbag.

'Crikey! What do you keep in there?' he says, swinging it over to her. 'Concrete blocks?'

'Never you mind,' she says. Then she stretches and twists so she can buckle it round her waist. 'A true lady never reveals her secrets.'

Daniel and Monkey

– I don't like this, D-Unit, says Monkey as we drive along the road. It is still almost dark.

— Why not? I ask.

— You grow up in the jungle, you learn to watch out for snakes. Know what I'm sayin'?

— I thought you grew up in NEW YORK CITY.

Monkey shakes his head and says, Jeez. I'm talking about the concrete jungle. And the snakes? Forget it. Why do I gotta . . . ?

I gulp because I'm worried that Monkey is MAD at me. He's NEVER mad at me normally.

Monkey sighs and he says, Ah, I'm sorry. I got a pain where my tail used to be — it's the cold air, y'know. And I'm worried, man.

He gives me a hug and the white starts to come back.

— Would you like to play DINOSAUR HUNTERS? I say.

Monkey lays his head on my tummy. Sure, buddy. Whatever you want, he says, and I blink three times and suddenly we are in a hot steamy place, next to a bubbling lake with an erupting volcano in the distance and we are sitting in our DinoMobile which is like a ten-year-old Citroën Grand Picasso but with force fields and anti-T-rex windows.

— Is that an Argentinosaurus, which is the HEAVIEST dinosaur you will ever meet? I say and I feel Pink as well as White.

But Monkey doesn't answer so I tickle him and he says, Sorry, man. You play without me. I'd better keep lookout.

But I can't play without Monkey, and the hot steamy place and the Pink disappears and I am back in a normal car, looking out of a normal window.

Megan

We've been ploughing along the motorway for about twenty minutes. It still feels like something very strange is going on.

The traffic's quite heavy but Dad's happy, whistling in the front. Mum is frantically ticking books with her green pen, while scrolling through emails on her iPad with the other hand. Occasionally she steals a gulp from the coffee cup that's wedged between her leg and the door.

There's a junction ahead.

'Wrong lane,' Mum says, glancing up. 'You want to come off here.'

'Uh-huh,' says Dad, not slowing down or moving across.

'Did you hear me?' she says a few seconds later. 'School's up there.'

'Got you . . .' he replies, but now we're almost up to the

junction and – yep – we've passed it. I watch it disappear behind us.

So does Mum. 'What are you doing? We're heading towards Manchester now!'

'Mmmm,' says Dad.

'Stop messing about. I've got a meeting at quarter to eight that I've got to prepare for.'

'Meeting's cancelled,' Dad says.

There's a pause.

I raise an eyebrow.

'What?' says Mum.

Dad slows down for some roadworks. 'You're currently sat on the toilet with . . . you know . . . *diarrhoea*.'

Mum leans forward. 'Excuse me?'

'I called in sick for you and left a message on the school answerphone. Sorry, by the way – I had to use the word "explosive".'

'Are you serious?' she yells. 'You *phoned* my school to tell them I've got . . . *explosive* diarrhoea? What is wrong with you?'

'Think yourself lucky. I *so* nearly said "volcanic".'

Gross.

'Oooh, I'd love to have explosive diarrhoea,' says Grandma dreamily.

I'm pretty sure that nobody has ever said this sentence before.

'I haven't been since Thursday,' Grandma continues, completely unnecessarily. 'It's like a traffic jam in a tunnel.' *Urgh.*

'Oh. My. God,' Mum says, running her fingers through her hair. 'Turn this car round right now and take me straight to work. I'll tell them it's a mistake. It's a joke. It's . . .'

'Can't,' says Dad. 'You've got to take forty-eight hours off for a tummy bug. If it turns out to be a bad one, we might be able to keep you off till Friday.'

'A bad one?' says Mum. 'What are you on about? It doesn't exist.'

'Your school thinks it does,' says Dad.

A vein in Mum's forehead begins throbbing. 'So I suppose you hid my car keys as well?'

'Kind of,' says Dad. Then he clears his throat. 'Which means, yes, I did. Sorry for that too.'

'But why?'

Dad chooses not to reply to that one.

'And what about Megan?' Mum asks. 'How's *she* supposed to get to school?'

'She's got a highly contagious crusty skin condition,' he explains.

There's a long silence. Then Mum tuts to herself. 'Why couldn't *I* have had a crusty skin condition?'

Nobody's ever said this sentence before either.

'Come on,' replies Dad. 'The people at your school

know that you'd still be at work if your head fell off. I
figured it had to be dramatic. I might've got a bit carried
away though. Sorry.'

'I'll never live this down,' she says. 'I'll get the sack. And
then we'll really be in trouble. I'm hanging onto this job by
a thread as it is.'

'No, you're not,' says Dad. 'They know you've got a lot
on your plate.'

'Speaking of plates,' says Grandma. 'Will there be food
where we're going?'

Trust her.

'Oh yes,' says Dad. 'Plenty.'

'Good,' says Grandma. 'I mean, I've got snacks for myself
in my bumbag. But I wouldn't want the rest of you going
hungry.'

We're in a service-station cafe. Grandma's shuffled off to
the shop. Mum's on her phone somewhere. Her second
coffee of the day is going cold on the table next to her
empty chair.

Daniel and I are sort of sharing a flapjack – as in I'm
eating my bit and he's glaring at his like he wants to beat
it up.

'This is great, isn't it?' says Dad to me, super-cheerful.

'You're always moaning that we never get to go on holiday.'

I bite my lip. 'I complained *once*.'

It did sometimes used to annoy me: we've never been able to go away like other families because Daniel can't cope with unfamiliar bedrooms and strange-smelling houses. All of our days out have to be Daniel-friendly too – not too busy, not too noisy, and only ever to places that *he* wants to visit (and if I ever have to go to another Lego exhibition I swear I'll build a demolition truck out of plastic blocks and smash the whole place to bits). Even then he sometimes ends up having a meltdown the moment we arrive and we all have to get back in the car and drive straight home.

But I've always tried not to moan about it. That's Daniel. You can't have the funny, lovely part of him without also having the sensitive, moody part that flips out every time the world doesn't make sense to him. And *this* – Daniel being so spaced out that he doesn't care – is a million times worse than not going on holiday.

I just want my brother back.

'What are we doing, Dad?' I ask eventually.

'I'll explain when your mum gets back. But here – this is where we're going . . .'

He gets his phone out of his pocket and pulls up the map. We're a blue, pulsing dot, somewhere near Leeds. The dot is on a long line that stretches right across the country, from our house in the north-west to a red pointer on the east coast.

It couldn't be further away from home without being in the sea.

Dad tilts the phone away from me and towards Daniel. Before the accident, Daniel always used to love watching the little blue dot creeping along as we drove somewhere.

'Check it out, Big D,' says Dad.

Daniel's eyes don't even move towards the screen.

Right then, Mum comes back and flops down. She looks pale and worried. 'Just spoke to my boss. I had to lie to him and pretend I was at home,' she says to Dad in a *this is all your fault* voice.

'What did he say?' asks Dad.

'He said he's not surprised I'm ill. Said I should've asked for some time off ages ago. He's signed me off for the whole week, and more if I need it.'

She takes a big, sad gulp of her coffee, and looks like she's about to cry.

I can't believe this. Is she mental? If someone had given me a week off I'd be doing somersaults.

'That's great!' says Dad, putting his hand on hers.

She brushes him off. 'What's so great about it? What if they decide they don't need me *at all* any more? Then we're stuffed.'

'That's not going to happen.'

'How do you know? You've risked my job, and you've kidnapped us.'

'Not kidnapped,' he says. 'Just *borrowed*.'

'Whatever. But you've still not told me what this is about.'

Dad takes a deep breath. He reaches into his woolly jacket and pulls out Daniel's notebook.

'"Chip Shop Challenge"?' reads Mum, squinting at the cover. 'What's that got to do with anything?'

He opens it at a page with a folded-down corner and holds it up for us. 'Remember this? I cut it out for Daniel and stuck it in.'

It's a magazine article. Most of the type is so small I can't read it this far away. But the headline is big and bold, and I remember it straight away:

THE TOP FIVE CHIP SHOPS IN THE COUNTRY

Daniel showed it to us the night of the accident, just before we went out.

'What about them?' Mum says suspiciously.

Dad closes the notebook. 'I thought we should visit all of them.'

'Whoa. Let me get this straight,' says Mum, putting

down her coffee. 'You phone me in sick and drag me across the country so we can *go to the chippy*? What is wrong with you?'

'It's not like that,' he says.

'Talk about stupid. And fish and chips? Are you serious?' says Mum.

We haven't eaten fish and chips since *that night*.

'Listen,' says Dad, grabbing her shoulder. 'What was it the doctor said: stimulation? Get his senses working?'

'You said the doctor was a brainless quack and you wouldn't trust her to treat a farting rabbit,' says Mum.

Dad pretends he hasn't heard her. 'Well, how about smell and taste? And maybe his memory too. Get him to remember. I can't believe we've never tried it till today.'

'Course we haven't,' snaps Mum. 'The last time we went for fish and chips . . .'

Her voice tails away.

Dad stirs a third sugar into his coffee. 'We need this. I realised last night. We should take some time out. Go to all five. Find the best one in the country. Just like I promised Daniel we would.'

'What are we going to wear?' I ask. I'm not spending a week in my school uniform without a change of pants.

'I packed bags for everyone last night from the stuff in the laundry basket,' he says without looking at me. 'They're in the boot.'

'Oh, *that's* what all the banging was about,' says Mum.

I dread to think what clothes he might've brought for me.

Mum takes a drink then pulls a face. 'This is ridiculous. We've haven't had so much as a night away since Daniel was a baby.'

'Exactly,' says Dad. 'It's time we spent some time as a family. And if it wasn't for fish and chips . . .

'We'd have never been born,' I finish softly.

Mum doesn't join in.

'And what about that punky girl who pinched my chip twenty years ago, eh?' says Dad, clasping Mum's hands. 'She'd have done it.'

'That was a long time ago,' says Mum.

'Look. We've got to try to help Daniel.'

'I am *trying to help him*,' says Mum. 'That's why he needs to stay at that clinic!'

'No. He. Needs. To. Be. With. Us.'

Mum puts her head in her hands.

'Listen to me,' says Dad. 'It's fate. I can't believe I'd forgotten to tell you. There was a reason why I cut out that article in the first place. A reason why I promised Daniel we'd visit all of them.'

'I don't want to hear it,' she says, waving her hand to silence him.

'Suit yourself. It'll be a surprise then,' says Dad, before

turning to me. 'Megan. Help me out here.'

I nearly choke on my flapjack. Someone is actually asking *me* what *I* think. Bring out the brass band and put up the flags.

I don't really know what to say. I mean, part of me wonders what the point of being together is when we're such a mess. It's not like we're going to have a good time.

Then I look at Daniel – those big brown eyes, those curly eyelashes, that scruffy hair, that duffel coat. That Monkey.

It's still Daniel in there. Or at least it still *looks* like him. I can't have him two hundred miles away from me. The closest we've ever come to not sleeping under the same roof was when I went to Brownie camp when I was eight. Daniel had such a tantrum that Dad had to come and get me. I hadn't even finished toasting my marshmallow on the campfire.

'I guess it's worth a try,' I offer, my throat dry.

After what seems like ages, Mum sucks her teeth. 'It's not like you're going to turn back, is it?'

Dad claps. 'Aha! Fant—'

'But one condition,' she interrupts. 'The second anything goes wrong, I'm phoning that clinic straight away. Got it?'

'That's not fair,' says Dad.

Mum shrugs. 'That's the deal.'

Dad runs his fingers through his messy greying hair. 'You can phone them when there's no hope left.'

Mum nods.

'So,' I say, 'Are we going to the chippy then?'

But, before anyone can answer, Daniel ruins everything.

Daniel and Monkey

— But I'm HUNGRY. Why CAN'T I eat the flapjack? I say to Monkey.

He is looking around the place, all suspicious and worried, which is making me Purple NERVOUS.

— I already said to ya. Don't take nothin' off 'em till we know what their game is, you get me?

— Not really, I say.

— Just tryin' to keep us safe, big guy, says Monkey.

— From what?

— I dunno what gives, man, but somethin' real freaky's goin' on. Like, what we doin' here? Why we driving?

My belly grumbles so I reach forward to pick up the flapjack, but Monkey slaps me on the hand quite hurty.

— Ow! I say and the flapjack lands on the floor.

— Never do that again, ya hear me! Never! It might be a trap!

I don't like it when he shouts and I pull my hood RIGHT UP over my face and YANK the toggles SUPER-TIGHT and I keep saying sorry sorry sorry and he says, C'mon. Give my hand a kiss. You're lucky I'm here, D-Unit. Lucky I'm here.

Your Guide to the Best Fish and Chip Shops in the UK

5) Frying Nemo – Norfolk

Nothing says traditional British seaside fun like a steaming tray of fish and chips as the sun goes down. With its epic portions and low prices, it's no wonder that this cheap and cheerful chip shop has been packed out with holidaymakers for over fifty years. So pull up a deckchair, put your knotted hanky on your head and enjoy the best beachfront grub in the country. Just don't expect to fit into your bikini tomorrow . . .

Megan

It feels like we've been driving for about eleven years, but the map on my phone shows we're nearly here. Dad shared it to my phone so I could show Daniel, but he's not bothered.

We pass a green sign:

Welcome to Great Yarmouth

I've never been this far away from home before. It seems like a seriously long way to go for fish and chips.

I *want* this to work. I *want* it to make Daniel better. I *want* our family to be back to normal.

But I just don't see how it can.

Back at the service station, Daniel looked like he was about to eat his flapjack. But then he slapped it out of his hand with Monkey and it went bouncing across the floor. Since then he's been really agitated – constantly muttering to Monkey and sucking its hand.

Mum's spent the whole time emailing and stressing about work, and Grandma's been her usual self. I do love her, really I do, but she's seriously annoying when she wants to be.

Imagine three hours of this:

'Megan. Can you bite the peanuts out of these sweets? They play merry hell with my teeth.'

'But they're PEANUT M&Ms, Grandma. Why did you buy them if you don't like peanuts?'

'Well, they're bigger than the ones *without* peanuts in.'

'Yeah – because they're ninety per cent peanut.'

'That's why I want you to take them out. And don't you be eating any of them. I need them for my sugar levels. I'm a sick woman. I've got a faulty valve and cysts on the walls of my spleen, you know . . .'

'Are they real things?'

'Course they are. I read about them in my magazine.'

We pull into a large, almost empty car park opposite the Pleasure Beach, which seems to be shut. No carriages are speeding up and down the roller coaster, and there are no screams coming over the fences. There's something quite sad about this, I think, especially since Dad promised he'd go on a ride with me.

Dad rubs his hands together. 'Right then! Frying Nemo, here we come!'

At least this is a bit of a boost. I'm starving!

Daniel and Monkey

Ever since the flapjack, Monkey has been in a quiet mood, not very talky, which is not nice for me because I love him so much. I even asked him if his tail was sore earlier because sometimes he is sad because of his TERRIBLE ACCIDENT but he said he did NOT want to talk about it.

We get out of the car. I can smell the SEA, which is a NICE SMELL and makes me feel Pink, even though I don't like swimming in the sea because it is cold and there are fishes there that might bite your toe off or SWIM UP YOUR WILLY.

Then Monkey says, Hey! Pay attention. We gotta be real careful here, buddy.

And I say, Why?

And he says, I don't trust these chumps. Stay close to your old pal Monkey, got it?

And I say, OK.

And so off we go and we are WALKING ALONG. But then I start THINKING A THINK. And the more I walk, the more I THINK. And the more I THINK, the more it starts BUGGING ME.

— Monkey, I say.

And he says, yeah, man.

I have a bit of PHLEGM in my THROAT so I cough it up. Then I say, I'm wondering how I know I'm scared of the sea when I've never been in it before.

And as I say this I realise it is QUITE A BIG THING.

I mean, how do I know ANYTHING at all?

And then I realise that this is actually a VERY, VERY BIG THING. How do I even know Monkey's name? I don't remember him ever telling me it.

But then again — I think — he IS a Monkey.

But then again AGAIN — I think — how do I know what a monkey is in the first place?

It is like I am having an ARGUMENT with myself inside my SKULL and I DON'T LIKE IT and I start to feel a bit Orange WORRIED.

And I notice that Monkey is staring at me. His eyes are open really wide like a surprised person in a cartoon.

Then he says, I don't know how comes you're scared o' the sea. Maybe you had a dream or somethin'.

His voice is quite growly.

— Yes. That must be it, I say, and I try to get rid of the THINK because it's making my BRAIN HURT.

Megan

'We've passed six chip shops already,' wheezes Grandma. 'My legs'll be worn away to stumps at this rate.'

Her stick goes *kajunk-kajunk* along the tarmac, and her bumbag jangles with every step.

'But it's GOT to be the one from the list,' says Dad, striding off ahead of us. He's got his old, determined bounce back. 'Not much further now.'

There's a ghostly atmosphere in the town. You can tell it'd be a fun place to have a holiday in the summer – amusement arcades, cafes, shops, a lovely long beach – but it's November so all the tourists must've gone home and half the shops are closed.

Not that we've ever been a beach family. The closest we got was a day out in Blackpool last year. Dad tried to take Daniel for a paddle, and Daniel liked the idea of it. Then the cold water splashed his feet and he lost it completely, tearing off up the beach like he'd just been sprayed with acid. Apparently he'd seen a TV show about fish that swim up your *you-know-what* and it all got too much for him.

Anyway, it all seems a bit miserable here today. The few places that are open have got hardly anyone in them – bored-looking old people blowing on their cups of tea, or kids who probably should be in school bashing the buttons on arcade machines. The grey, drizzly weather isn't helping either. Even the fat seagulls look sad as they peck the pavement looking for scraps.

After about half a mile, Dad spots a sign up ahead. 'Look! There it is! Frying Nemo!'

I'm surprised at how happy I feel. It's like we've achieved something. It's taken us all day but we've made it. The light rain and chill wind suddenly don't feel unpleasant – they're sweet and bracing. We cross the road from the prom and all of us – even Grandma and Daniel – pick up the pace.

For the last ten metres or so Dad does that silly slow-motion run he used to do to make Daniel laugh. He's so embarrassing sometimes. I cringe and glance up and down the road to make sure nobody else is watching.

Arms raised like a marathon winner crossing the line, he reaches the steps, breathing in and out hard.

Then he frowns. His face drops, and so do his arms.

'What is it?' says Mum.

Dad doesn't answer.

The rest of us draw level with him. There's a sign stuck inside the glass door, right underneath the same magazine cut-out that Daniel's got in his notebook:

Sorry were closed!
Thank's for you're custom.

We're off to Spain til it get's warmer!
See you next summer!

The spelling mistakes and badly used apostrophes seem to make it even worse.

'No,' says Dad. 'It can't be.'

He leans forward and slaps his hands against the metal door frame. For a second I think he's going to punch a hole in the window, but then he just slumps down on the step.

Mum gets there and reads the sign herself. 'Oh.'

Dad doesn't answer her. His head is in his hands.

'Karen,' says Grandma, finally catching up. 'I say, Karen, is there a toilet? All this walking's jiggled something loose.'

Why does she have to be so *gross*?

'It's closed,' says Mum.

'Closed?' says Grandma. 'Have you tried the door? Maybe they've nipped out for five minutes.'

'They've gone to Spain.'

'Well, how will they be back in five minutes then?'

'They didn't say they w—'

'I could really do with the loo, Karen.'

Mum ignores her. 'We can go to one of the other chip shops on the seafront,' she says, a kind hand on Dad's shoulder. I'm a bit surprised she's not cross with him. 'The one by the car park with the green sign looked nice.'

'But it *needs* to be *this* one,' says Dad, heels of his hands jammed into his eyes. It's amazing how much he reminds me of Daniel right now. 'We're meant to find the best one. That's the whole point.'

Hmm, I think. I know Dad's got a list and everything, but how do we know that this list has the best five on it? There must be thousands of chip shops in the country. Who could possibly say which ones are best? I'm wondering whether there's any point mentioning this when I realise something.

'Hey!' I say. My heart feels like it might burst out of my ribcage. 'Where's Daniel?'

Daniel and Monkey

We were walking along this path with no cars and a big wall to keep the sea out and the wind all blustery and wet and Monkey kept telling me he didn't like it.

Then we crossed the road with the people and they walked off and I saw some TWINKLY LIGHTS and I said, Hey look, Monkey, and we went into the place with the TWINKLY LIGHTS and it gave me a really nice white feeling like getting out of the bath with a fluffy towel.

So now we're standing and looking at the twinkly lights and there are coins and this thing like a moving shelf with REAL MONEY on it, and if you stare at it your eyes go all funny.

— We need to get away, says Monkey, and I look at him instead of at the coins.

— Get away? I say. I'm not sure why, but the way he says it gives me a STRANGE FEELING in my tummy.

Monkey opens his mouth to speak but then he seems to change his mind. After a while he SMILES very nice and he says, I mean like go to space.

— YESSSSSS! I say because I've wanted to do a FUN GAME with Monkey ALL DAY.

— Best thing about space, you don't see nobody else, right? he says.

— Right.

— Monkey and Daniel, alone and together forever.

And just like that we are in a BRILLIANT SPACECRAFT which has got loads of amazing things in it like FLASHING LIGHTS and BUTTONS and big windows that you can see STARS and ASTEROIDS out of, and LASER GUNS, and we are floating because that's what it's like in ZERO GRAVITY.

— Commander Daniel, says Monkey, who is wearing

a silver SPACESUIT and a BIG HELMET and looking
at a screen.

— Yes, Space Admiral Monkey, I say.

— An alien spacecraft from the Planet Spud is
trying to zap us.

— Engage death rays.

Pyew-pyew.

— It's no use! They're getting closer! What shall
we do, Commander?

And I take charge, which is what SPACE
COMMANDERS do, and I say, There's only one thing
for it: hold on for HYPERSPACE!

— If we don't get through this, I want you to
know that I love you, Commander, says Space
Admiral Monkey.

— And I love you too, I say, and I kiss his hand.

Then I push a BIG RED BUTTON and we're
thrown backwards and there's a sound like
PNNNEEEYYYYYOOOOOWWW and the stars turn
into white lines going past the spaceship. Then
there's a BRIGHT FLASH and everything disappears.

Megan

We're all seriously panicking.

Dad: 'I thought he was with *you.*'

Mum: 'You check over the sea wall. I'll go in the shops. Megan – the seafront.'

Grandma: 'I'll have a look in the ladies' toilets over there I could do with going anyway.'

Then – almost straightaway – I find him. He's just inside the doorway of the arcade next door, his face pressed to the window of one of the tuppenny shove machines.

'He's in here!' I call out, relief pouring through me.

It's weird – before the accident he'd have run a mile from an arcade: all that noise and those flashing lights would've tipped him over the edge.

Mum and Dad bundle him up into their arms, squeezing him tightly. I try to join in but I'm outside the group hug. *At least he's safe,* I think, but there's a bitter taste in the back of my mouth.

'Gave us a fright, Big D.'

'Don't ever do that again!'

But Daniel doesn't move. He just stands there, arms stiff, Monkey peeping out at me over the crook of his elbow.

Daniel and Monkey

I am being squashed by the people and the people are saying WAARK WAARK WAARK!

It's NOT NICE because I don't like being SQUASHED and I don't like the NOISE of the people YABBERING on. But it's a BIT NICE too because something about it is SAFE and TIGHT, like when you zip a sleeping bag up to your chin.

And then I think, HANG ON. What is a sleeping bag? And I've got that FUNNY FEELING again that I'm REMEMBERING something that I've NEVER SEEN BEFORE.

But then Monkey says, We shoulda gone for real when we had the chance, buddy.

He says it in a SQUEEZY voice because he's being STRANGLED.

And I stop thinking about the SLEEPING BAG and I start wondering what he means.

Megan

After what seems like ages, Grandma comes out of the public loo. 'Ooh, that seat was cold,' she says. 'And there was no paper. Lucky I had loo roll in my bumbag.'

'Surprised she didn't have a whole toilet in there,' says Dad. 'She could fit one.'

He's cheered up at least.

'Are we getting chips or what?' asks Grandma.

Mum and Dad glance at each other, unsure.

Just then, Daniel starts grunting and muttering excitedly, with Monkey close up in front of his face again.

Daniel and Monkey

– Did you just say CHIPS? I say to Monkey.

Straight away he's in front of my face, really close. He looks very SERIOUS.

– What? he says.

– I heard someone say chips, I say.

A few seconds ago he was talking about running away, but then I'm SURE he said CHIPS, and I feel a funny BUZZY feeling in my brain.

Monkey gulps. Then he coughs. Then he says, Sure thing, buddy. It was me. I said chips.

When he says the word CHIPS again, the BUZZY feeling gets BIGGER. My tummy starts to go CRACKERJACK and now I am licking my lips and I start to have a PICTURE IN MY BRAIN OF . . .

— Whatcha doin? says Monkey.

— Nothing, I say super-quick, because for some reason I think I shouldn't tell Monkey what I was thinking about. The picture in my head DISAPPEARS before I can see it properly and I feel a little bit SAD that it has gone but I don't know WHY.

— Y'know WHY I said . . . THAT WORD? says Monkey, fiddling with his hands like he's THINKING HARD.

— Why? I ask.

— Because — I — uh — I wanna change my name.

I'm not thinking about the picture in my head any more because I'm getting the Orange which means SCARED or WORRIED because I don't like things to change and Monkey's ALWAYS been Monkey since FOREVER.

— What's wrong with the name Monkey?

— It . . . er . . . don't make me feel like an individual.

— I don't get what you MEAN.

– How'd ya like to be called Boy? Or Human?

There are real sad CRYING TEARS dripping from under Monkey's sunglasses. So as well as the Orange, I've got Turquoise, which is the GUILTY feeling when you've done something wrong and you feel bad.

He says, all croaky, I need people to know who I am. I lost my tail, man. I don't feel like myself no more.

When he gets sad I get sad, so even though I DON'T want him to change his name, I say, What name are you thinking of?

And Monkey says, with suddenly NO MORE TEARS, Chips. My new name is Chips. THAT'S why I said it before, see – I was testing it out.

– Chips? I say, a bit laughy, which is nice after the Orange and Red and Turquoise, even though it's STRANGE how he could make his tears stop so quickly.

Monkey bites his lip. No. Not Chip-suh with an S. That's somethin' you shouldn't be thinkin' about. I said Chip-zuh with a zee.

He calls it a zee because he is American from New York City. I feel frowny and I say, But why shouldn't I think of the word CHIPS? And why do you need a ZED in your NAME?

I call it a zed because I'm NOT American from New York City.

Monkey pulls on the lapels of his leather jacket and wiggles his sunglasses up and down and says, A zee makes a name cooler, doncha think? Wouldn't you put a zee in your name if ya could?

— Zaniel? I say.

He didn't explain why I shouldn't think about CHIPS with an S.

— Nah. Maybe not. But I want ya to call me Chipz from now on. With a zee.

I screw up my face, which means I'm NOT SURE.

He says, Ah, c'mon, man. You're meant to be my buddy. Unless you ain't my buddy no more. Is that it?

And he looks sad, so I say, Daniel and Chipz! DANIEL and CHIPZ!

— Shhh, man. Keep it down. We don't want no one to hear.

And I squeeze him tight because we are SUPER-PALS, and even though I don't like it I'll still call him Chipz, because that's what FRIENDS DO and I need to make him happy after his TERRIBLE ACCIDENT.

— You're a good kid, says Monkey I mean Chipz into my ear.

Megan

My heart is do ng proper backflips. 'Mum! Dad! Did you hear that? Did you hear him?'

'Hear what?' says Mum, who's a few steps in front of me.

'He said words!'

His voice was quiet and dry like someone who's not had a drink in a week, but they were real, proper words. Again! Twice in two days.

I'm totally flapping now and my brain is spinning and spinning. I feel like Daniel when he's got the Blue or something.

'Who said words?' says Grandma, from behind me, which is just about the dumbest question ever so I don't bother answering it.

'I heard . . . *something*,' says Dad, like he's trying not to get too excited.

And I'm looking at Daniel but he's silent again, pulling the collar of his duffel coat up over his face.

'He said Daniel! And then he said *chips*,' I say. 'So it's obvious. We need to get Daniel some chips.'

'Look! There's another chippy just over the road!' says Mum, excited.

'Let's do it!' says Dad. He doesn't seem to care any more that we only go to ones from the list.

'The Bulldog Chip Shop?' I say doubtfully, taking in the shabby sign and the peeling paintwork. 'Are you sure?'

I don't like the look of it but we're in a rush. It's like someone's cleaned Daniel's windscreen. We've got to get the chips before it fogs up again.

Even from here we can tell it's only a small place with no tables, so Daniel, Mum and Grandma huddle on a bench looking out to sea, while Dad and I trot back across the main road.

As soon as we step inside I know it's a mistake.

Everything about it is bad.

There are no customers, and a bell rings when we walk in. Good chip shops don't need a bell – they're never empty so the staff are always ready. Plus it's uncomfortably hot in here after being out in the rain, and the fat in the air is clinging to my lungs like tar.

I look around uneasily. It hasn't been cleaned in a while. The walls are splattered with grease and covered with handwritten signs that say things like: 'Got a problem? Contact our complaints department!' with an arrow pointing to an overflowing bin.

Nobody comes out to serve us. We stare at the dangly metal chain curtain that hangs in the doorway to the back room.

'Maybe we *should* go to one of the ones further along?' I say.

'No,' says Dad, wiggling his foot so the coins jangle in his pocket. 'We need this. Now. While Daniel's talking.'

A skinny woman with her hair scraped back emerges through the dangly metal curtain. She says nothing. Just stares at us. It's like she's never seen a human before and, having finally seen one, she's decided that she doesn't really like them.

Dad swallows. 'Three portions of chips, please.'

'And two empty trays so we can share them out,' I say.

Still staring suspiciously at us, she tilts her head back. 'BRYAN!' she suddenly bellows, louder than a fire alarm. I nearly jump out of my skin. Her mouth is massive and she only has about six teeth.

No reply.

'BRY-AN!' she repeats, somehow even louder.

'Bloody 'ell, woman. What d'you want?' comes a gruff reply, as a man stumbles out through the curtain. He's wearing a filthy white jacket, open all the way down, and he's doing up the buttons on his jeans with his stubby fingers.

Gross.

Rule one about serving food must surely be: *Don't let the customer know you've just been to the bog.* He doesn't look like a hand-washer to me.

'HOW LONG ARE THE CHIPS GONNA BE, BRYAN?' shrieks the woman. She's still staring at us, and she hasn't lowered the volume even though Bryan is now standing right next to her massive gob.

Before BRYAN! can answer (I imagine there's an exclamation mark on his birth certificate), I lean over the counter and hold out my finger and thumb. 'About three to four centimetres, I expect.'

Couldn't resist. I just wanted to make Dad laugh but, when I look at him, his face is serious.

The two mutants behind the counter don't get the joke anyway. They look at me like I've just miaowed at them.

'Ten minutes,' grunts BRYAN! He does up the last button on his jeans. 'We've not put any in yet.'

They carry on staring at us.

They haven't made any chips yet? I know it's off-season, but there *are* people about *and* it's tea time, but they've not had a single customer? What's wrong with this place? What do other people know that we don't?

'Maybe one of the other shops will be ready to serve us . . . ?' I say, pulling Dad's sleeve.

'No,' says Dad. 'We'll wait.'

Is he nuts?

It takes ages for BRYAN! to sort out the chips. The whole time the woman stares at us, like she thinks we're going to pinch something. There's nothing to steal though, unless you count the yellowing, three-month-old newspapers on the windowsill with the headlines 'Aliens Nicked My Knickers!' and 'Man Trapped in Lift Eats Own Willy to Survive!' or the dead wasps lying on top of them.

'Three fifty-five,' she snaps at us when BRYAN! plonks the chips on the counter. This can't be the price for three portions of chips; it doesn't divide by three. There isn't a price list or menu on the wall though, just a load of badly spelled day-glo signs, like: 'SASUAGES – NOW WITH MORE MEET'.

'And another three quid for the extra trays,' says BRYAN!

'Really?' I splutter. *Rip-off!*

Dad waves his hand at me to say, *Forget it.* 'Five tomato ketchups too.'

'Another two pound,' says the woman. She plonks a fistful of them on the counter. The metal surface has a grimy pattern from being wiped with a dirty cloth.

I pick up one of the sachets and look at the label.

There's a picture of squirrel in a stethoscope, with 'Doctor Sauce's Tomato-Style Ketchup' written above it.

What the hell is tomato-*style* ketchup? Surely something's either tomato ketchup or it isn't. What have they made it with if they haven't used tomatoes? Is that what the squirrel's all about? Has someone *juiced* a squirrel?

I bet it's horrible. And 40p a pop for squirrel juice? Is she having a laugh?

Dad takes a deep breath and starts counting out his coins.

Back at the bench, Dad starts sharing the chips into the five trays. They're pale, wet and floppy, and the grease is disgusting. If I wasn't so hungry I'd just bin them.

'Were there no forks?' says Grandma. 'I need a fork. A woman my age can't go round with greasy fingers. What would people say?'

'Have you not got one in your bumbag?' asks Dad, dumping a handful of chips into a tray.

I thought he was joking, but Grandma slips the key from round her neck, unlocks the padlock and starts rummaging inside. I try to see what she's got in there – folded bits of paper, a purse, her loo roll, a bag of sweets – but she notices me looking and quickly turns to the side to hide it from me. After a few moments she produces a metal knife and fork. 'Aha!' she says, quickly zipping it back up.

Incredible.

I tap Daniel on the shoulder. 'Hey, Snotface. Fancy some chips?'

He pushes Monkey up under his duffel coat, then yanks the hood down over his face.

Daniel and Chipz

— Quick. Under here. We gotta hide from 'em, says Monkey I mean Chipz, and we bury ourselves under my coat, which is DARK but COSY.

I know who he means. The people. Someone is talking — more nonsense like WAARK WAARK WAARK. Then there's one word I recognise: Chipz.

— Hey! Did you hear that? How FUNNY! Someone just said YOUR NAME! I say.

— Don't listen to 'em, D-Dog!

I nod but there is this really NICE SMELL coming from somewhere and I SNIFF the air.

— Hey. Hey. Hey, whatcha doin'? Don't you be smellin' that, says Chipz.

But I CAN'T stop smelling the smell because it is LOVELY and EVERYWHERE and I RECOGNISE it from somewhere and now there is something on my lap which is WARM and almost BURNY but not quite and I poke my head up over the top of my coat just to see what it is and from under my coat Chipz is saying, Come back here, man.

But I can't really HEAR him and I NEED to find out what that SMELL is.

Megan

Oh my word.

As soon as I put Daniel's tray on his lap, he popped his head out of his duffel coat and now his nose is twitching like a flipping meerkat.

'You want some chips?' I ask him, wafting the smell towards his face with my hand. *Stimulate his senses* – that's what the doctor said.

I squirt in some of the tomato-style squirrel juice, which comes out watery and brown. Then I dip a chip into it and hold it up to him.

'Remember, Snotface? Chips. Your favourite.'

He stares at it for ages. His forehead wrinkles. Eventually, and very slowly, he wriggles the rest of his face out of the top of his jacket. His mouth opens a tiny bit and I slide the chip inside.

Then everything changes.

He smiles.

Daniel and Chipz

Something is in my mouth and now I am chewing it and it tastes FANDABBYDOOZALICIOUS!

Oh, wow! Oh wow wow wow! Now I remember what the smell is — CHIPS! And now I remember what CHIPS are too. They are a DELICIOUS FOOD!

And that's so FUNNY because that is almost the same name as Monkey I mean Chipz just gave himself!

I remember SALT and VINEGAR and FAT and POTATO and it is making my mouth water and it tastes miles better because I have not had chips since . . . er . . . I don't remember.

Megan

'Oh my!' says Mum. 'He's smiling!'

'That's it, Big D. Have another,' says Dad, and Daniel greedily guzzles the chip out of Dad's fingers.

'Go on, Snotface,' I say, and there's a big lump in my throat.

It's the simplest thing in the world but it's so lovely. You always know exactly how Daniel's feeling. His face is so expressive. And now his eyes are closed, his cheeks are bulging, his mouth is moving round and round and he's making all these *nymm, nymm* noises.

'Not enough vinegar on these,' grumbles Grandma.

Daniel and Chipz

— Yo, yo, yo. Whatcha doing, Funky D-Meister? says Chipz, crawling out from under my duffel coat and sitting on my tummy. I LOVE it when he calls me Funky D-Meister or Disco Dan the Groovy Pant Man.

I show him the sloppy food in my mouth and I say, Hey, look! I just remembered what chips are. Like your name!

Chipz's forehead is crumpled up which is a frown. Someone taught me once that this means he might be CROSS like when I feel Red, so I swallow and say, Are you OK?

He takes a deep breath and then he says, Why you gotta eat the fries, man?

He says fries because that's what they say

in New York City.

And I say, Because I'm HUNGRY and they're
TASTY. Here. Try one.

— Get that away from me! says Monkey, and he
SWIPES my hand away.

— What's wrong? I say. Monkey I mean Chipz
never normally minds me eating food.

— You're busting my pipes, man, he says, VERY
angry now, and he's looking at me over his
sunglasses and shaking his head and it's HORRIBLE
because I've never seen him like this before EVER.

— What do you mean? I say, sad like the Grey is
coming. I drop a chip back into the tray.

— Eatin' the fries, man. That's what they want
you to do.

— Who?

He shakes his head again. Then he says, Doncha
get it, buddy? Doncha? Huh?

— No, I say, because I really do NOT and now I
am Orange scared too.

— I told ya. These schmucks want me out the
picture, and they'll do anything to trick ya.

And he hops off my leg and GRABS the tray of
chips.

— What are you doing? I ask.

— Sortin' out this mess.

And I let him take them because no matter HOW TASTY they are, I care more about CHIPZ with a ZED than I care about CHIPS with an S.

Megan

So one second he was eating the chips just fine. He even took a couple himself, laughing and making all these contented lip-smacking noises. And his mutterings sounded like they were almost about to turn into words. We all held our breath, mouths open, all silently urging him to say something.

Then suddenly he stopped. His face fell. He pulled Monkey out from under his coat and he started jabbering to it again – urgently, angrily. Then he screamed out, 'No! No! No!' And now he's picked up the tray of chips, holding it between Monkey's hands.

'Hey. What are you doing?' I ask him.

Just like that, he flings the tray away. Chips fly through the air, exploding across the pavement.

I feel my heart sink. Then I shudder. The sight of the chips on the tarmac reminds me so much of *that night*.

'Daniel!' says Mum.

Dad groans.

'Well, they might not be the best, but surely they're not *that* bad,' says Grandma. 'I'd have finished 'em for you.'

Daniel shuts his eyes tight, buries himself back under his duffel coat and cuddles Monkey.

Daniel

The chips have gone away which is sad and Grey, and I feel mad with the people for trying to trick me, which is Red. My breathing is HEAVY and RAGGEDY.

But then something else comes. It is Yellow, which is CONFUSED, because I have just thought of something: how could I know what CHIPS are when I don't REMEMBER when I had them before? It's like how I know about the sea and the sleeping bag — a total MYSTERY — and it makes me feel DIZZY and STRANGE.

Then Chipz cuddles up to the side of my face and says, Don't worry about it, big guy. Ya did the right thing.

Megan

We sit there for ages. Nobody says anything. Nobody eats. Nobody moves. A couple of manky seagulls start pecking at Daniel's chips. Then Mum screws up her tray and shoves it into the bin next to us. 'Right then. Five hours home. I don't mind driving.'

'Eh?' says Dad.

'I'll phone work. Maybe they'll let me in on Thursday,' says Mum. 'Then we'll call the doctor. Tell her that Daniel's ready for that clinic.'

'We're not going home yet,' says Dad, softly but firmly.

'He's right. We can't go home now,' says Grandma. 'I've not finished my chips.'

Mum ignores her. 'But you said when it fails . . .'

'And *you* said *only when there's no more hope*,' says Dad. 'He spoke. And he smiled. And he enjoyed the chips. That's more than he's done in six weeks. Surely that's *hope*, isn't it?'

Mum runs her fingers through her hair. 'The clinic's got the world's top experts . . .'

'Who don't know him or love him,' says Dad.

'That isn't enough,' says Mum.

I need to do something fast.

I unzip Daniel's coat.

'Say Chips, Snotface,' I hiss at him. 'Chips.'

He looks back at me blankly, Monkey pressed against his ear.

'Just say it and I'll get you more chips. I promise.'

Daniel and Chipz

— Did you say MORE CHIPS? I say.

— No, says Chipz, snappy.

— Someone said MORE CHIPS, I say.

I had my eyes closed, then someone was going WAARK WAARK WAARK and I didn't understand it, then someone said MORE CHIPS.

And now the word chips is in my head and it's like a VOLCANO trying to ERUPT out of my mouth.

— Hey, man. Don't you say that word, says Chipz, which is VERY STRANGE because that's his name.

And the word is going from my brain to my MOUTH but it's like my lips are GLUED TOGETHER and it won't come out which makes me Purple worried.

Megan

Time is frozen. Daniel screws up his eyes, his teeth grinding together. 'Chhh . . .' he growls, like it causes him immense pain. 'Chhhhhhhh . . .'

'Come on, Snotface,' I say. 'You can do it.'

I can tell he's trying as hard as he can but he can't get the sound out of his mouth. You can see the pressure building in him, his shoulders twitching and his face going red, until he howls like a dog in pain, smacking himself on the side of the head. Then he yanks up his zip, buries his head between his legs and is silent again, apart from his deep, scratchy breathing.

For a moment nobody says anything.

At first I think Mum's going to make us go home – insist that this is the final straw – but instead she takes a deep breath. 'Fine. We'll keep going. For now.'

'Nice one, Megan,' whispers Dad, placing his hand on my shoulder.

I blush. It's like someone's dancing inside my tummy.

Your Guide to the Best
Fish and Chip Shops in the UK

4) Steve's Fish Bar, Bedfordshire

This picturesque little chippy is an absolute must for any visitors to the nearby safari park. Roll out a rug and watch the cricket on the village green, or gobble down the scrumptious grub in your steamy car after a long day of animal-spotting. Three-time finalist in the National Fryers' Awards.

Megan

We spent last night in a little bed and breakfast on the edge of Great Yarmouth, the five of us squeezed into a family room, with Dad on the floor. It looked as if it hadn't been decorated since about 1953 and it smelled like neglected guinea pigs.

It was a weird place to spend our first holiday night together ever. I asked Dad if I could have a room on my own, or at least share with Mum, but he said we had to bunk in together to save money for the rest of the trip. I slept with a pillow wrapped around my head – Daniel was wittering away to Monkey all night, and Grandma was snoring and trumping like a gorilla.

Still, after a bacon butty and some orange juice this morning, everyone seems happy and now we're bombing along the road.

'Keep talking to him,' Dad said to me this morning when we got in the car. He shared the directions with me again so I could see the route on my phone.

I open up the map app and hold the screen towards Daniel. 'Look at the blue dot, Snotface. That's us. And this red arrow way over here is where we're going.'

The route's taking us west, to some place in the middle

of the country I've never heard of before. Dad says we can have a day out at a safari park while we're there, which might be fun, I guess.

Daniel stares at my phone. And I stare at him, searching for a sign that he can hear me like he heard me yesterday.

Do his pupils change size to focus on it? Does his forehead crumple a little bit in concentration? Is he sucking Monkey's hand just a tiny bit harder today, like he's trying to block me out?

If we can get through to him again, then maybe . . .

'We'll get you back one day,' I say softly.

But Daniel turns away to face the window, Monkey cuddled up to his chin. Then he starts whispering to it again.

It's hard to get my head round, but I actually feel *jealous* of Monkey. Like, seriously, why should *it* get to chat to Daniel all the time? Why should Daniel act like we don't exist and spend all his time with *it*?

I hate that monkey!

Then I rub my forehead and take a deep breath.

It's a cuddly toy.

I'm turning into Daniel.

Daniel and Chipz

— That map was COOL, wasn't it? I say.

— No, says Chipz. He hasn't spoken very much today.

— B—

— Why doncha look out the window, man?

I do as he tells me, but I think that the map WAS quite cool. I don't know what it was a map of, but I LIKED the ZIGGYZAGGY blue line and the GLOWING BLUE DOT.

The DOT and the LINE looked FAMILIAR to me, like I'd seen them before, but I get that thought RIGHT out of my head MEGA-QUICK.

Last night in bed I told Chipz that I'd been wondering about how come I know some things but I can't remember HOW I KNOW THEM. And, when I THINK about it, I can't ACTUALLY remember anything from before Monkey's TERRIBLE ACCIDENT.

He said that HE SHOULD DO THE THINKIN' FROM NOW ON, because THINKIN'S DANGEROUS and MY BRAIN'S GONNA GET US BOTH IN BIG TROUBLE and HE'S GOT ENOUGH TO WORRY

ABOUT WITHOUT WORRYING ABOUT ME TOO.

He still seems quite sad now so I'll try not to think too much ANY MORE.

Megan

It's taken almost three hours but we've got here OK: the safari park is in the countryside near a city called Milton Keynes, which is about halfway between London and Birmingham.

There was one awkward bit. We were passing quite close to Cambridge and Mum told Dad she wanted to go and have a look at the clinic that Daniel might end up staying at. Dad said nothing and put his foot on the accelerator. Mum hasn't really talked to him since.

Now we're crawling down a long driveway across a field, with huge pictures of monkeys and lions alongside it. The cool bag is by my feet. There are five bite-size portions of fish and chips inside it, which smell *fantastic*. According to the list in Daniel's notebook, they're from the fourth-best chip shop in Britain so I reckon they'll be pretty tasty too.

The chip shop was just down the road in the next village, a pretty little place with flowerpots outside. The owner was big, pink and completely bald – not even eyebrows. He looked like he might recently have been boiled.

We could've eaten at the tables and chairs by the window overlooking the duck pond, or even out on the grass, but Dad was in a mischievous, happy mood. He said, 'What's the fun in that? Time we had an adventure, right?' and insisted on sneaking our chips into the safari park.

As we reach the gates, there's a sign warning us to **KEEP DOORS AND WINDOWS CLOSED AT ALL TIMES** and **DO NOT FEED THE ANIMALS.**

Grandma looks at a big picture of a lion and says, 'I'm not sure I like lions. I've heard they prey on the old and the weak.'

'Ah, come on. You must have a tranquilliser gun somewhere in your bumbag,' says Dad.

'The contents of a lady's personal luggage are a private matter,' says Grandma primly.

Dad eases the car up towards the kiosk where you pay. 'Speaking of which, can you hide the children in there so they get in for free?'

Grandma sniffs. 'I'll hide you in a flaming body bag if you're not careful.'

Dad laughs as he pays, then winds up the window. A huge electronic gate slides open and we creep inside.

'Let's try and enjoy ourselves, shall we?' says Mum. Then she drops her voice. 'Since we don't seem to have any choice about it.'

I screw up my face.

'Once we're out of sight, we'll crack open the grub,' says Dad, ignoring Mum's last comment.

Daniel and Chipz

Chipz is still in a NOT VERY TALKY mood.

I've been doing well at NOT THINKING today, but something just happened and it's making me THINK again.

I don't think Chipz noticed, but the people in the car got out a few minutes ago and one of them came back carrying a COOL BAG which is actually good for keeping things HOT and not just COLD.

And now there is a faint but VERY SPECIAL SMELL in the car that is getting STRONGER all the time and it smells a lot like those CHIPS from yesterday and it is making my belly bounce about like a GIANT JUMPING JELLY BEAN and I'm feeling a little bit Blue excited.

Suddenly Chipz sits up and he says, Hey, yo, D-Lite. We need to get outta here.

— Really? I say because I LIKE it here with the smell and part of me wants to see if there ARE chips, even though I will go WHEREVER he tells me to.

He tries the door but it is locked.

– Dammit, he says, which is a nasty swear word.

Then someone in the car grabs Chipz and starts saying, WAARK WAARK WAARK!

And I shout, Get off him!

Then they let go and I pull him into my chest SUPER-TIGHT.

Megan

'All right. Calm down, Snotface,' I say, holding my hands up away from him. 'I just didn't want you to escape, that's all.'

He scrunches himself up against the door, Monkey tucked under his armpit.

Luckily we always have the child lock on – when Daniel was little he used to try to make a run for it when we were waiting at traffic lights.

'Did he just say *dammit*?' asks Mum.

'Dunno. I didn't hear him,' I say. I was too busy trying to save his life.

Dad snorts with laughter. 'That's my boy!'

'Why don't you look out at the animals instead?' I say to

Daniel as we snake our way into the first field.

He glares out of the window, nervously clutching Monkey with its hand in his mouth.

Daniel and Chipz

Chipz seems like he's got a Purple mood, which is nervous. I can tell this because he is WIGGLING his legs and BITING his lip. I kiss his hand to calm him down.

— If we can't escape properly, then we gotta do something, he says.

— Like what?

— You wanna go on safari? To Africa?

And I am SUPER-BRIGHT PINK HAPPY because I was worried he was CROSS with me so I say YES, PLEASE!

And as if by MAGIC we are driving in a field and there are animals everywhere like rhinos and wildebeest which look like mean, muscly cows with massive horns, and Chipz and me are both wearing greeny-yellow shirts and shorts and long socks.

Chipz is LAUGHING and he says, Hey, D-Machine. Check out that zebra over there. It's taking a dump!

– Oh that is DISGUSTING! I say, but really it's HILARIOUS.

And then it gets even better because we go through a gate into another part of Africa and I can see some BABOONS.

Megan

'Look, Snotface!' I say. 'Monkeys.'

'Watch they don't pull off the windscreen wipers,' says Mum.

'Filthy beasts,' says Grandma, 'waggling their big red bottoms about. It's obscene. Someone ought to put underpants on them.'

Daniel is suddenly more alert than I've seen him in ages. He's staring out of the window, Monkey pressed against the glass.

Seeing the baboons out there makes me think a bit more about Monkey. What did that doctor say? *The monkey's a barrier, a shield, from the world. Have you tried removing it yet?*

I start to wonder what *would* happen if we did take it off him? I mean, properly.

We've not even tried since Dad got kicked in the nose.

Who's to say it wouldn't help him though? I mean, yeah, he'd get cross to start with. But if we could ride that out, maybe he'd get over it and then he'd be OK.

Hmm. Maybe one day.

The baboons come trotting over. One of them jumps on the roof with a *thudump*.

'Oi! Careful of the car,' says Dad. 'It's an antique.'

A couple of other baboons stare at us from the grass. One bares its sharp teeth as it gnaws on a bit of fruit from the ground.

I wish Monkey would jump out of the window and go and live with them.

I shake my head.

It's a cuddly toy. It's a cuddly toy.

'When can we have the chips?' I ask.

And Daniel slowly spins round to look at me.

Daniel and Chipz

— WAARK WAARK WAARK Chipz, says one of the people in the car.

I turn round QUICK-SHARP.

Was the person talking about my bestest friend CHIPZ or the tasty CHIPS that you eat but I'm not

going to think about because it's not RIGHT to?
But now that SMELL is getting EVEN STRONGER.

— Oooh ahhh, says Chipz all of a sudden, and I
turn back to him. His hand's on the hole on his
bottom where his tail should be.

— Are you OK? I say, Turquoise guilty and Purple
worried.

And Chipz says, No, man. I ain't. Seein' them
monkeys out there with their long tails . . . it
makes me realise what I lost.

I gulp because I WANT to focus on Chipz, but I
can't ignore that LOVELY SMELL.

— Makes me realise how much I need you . . . he
says.

I am licking my lips.

— Makes me realise that if you ever left me,
I'd be no better than them booty-scratchin'
buttheads out there, rollin' round in the dirt and
throwin' poop at cars.

And I want to tell him I love him but the smell
and the Turquoise and the Purple are so strong
that everything's getting too big and if I don't
do something NOW I'm going to EXPLODE so I put
my hands over my face and start making the
nnnngggggghhhh noise to BLOCK OUT THE SMELL.

Megan

'What's going on?' says Mum next to me.

'Everything OK back there?' asks Dad.

'Dunno,' I say quickly. 'Just drive.'

Dad honks his horn. The baboons scatter. The one on the roof jumps off. And we drive into the next field.

I hoped he might like seeing real-life monkeys instead of cuddly toy ones. I hoped it might bring him back into the real world a bit. I was wrong. He was fine till they came near us.

Now he's squashed right into the window, face covered.

There's one thing I can cling to though. When I said *chips,* he turned around. It's not much, but still – no matter what he did next – he heard me, and it gives me a little crackle of hope.

Maybe I can tempt him again?

I unzip the cool box and hand out the food. Fatty, vinegary warmth swirls round the car and fogs the windows. It's lovely.

For a moment, you could close your eyes, forget everything and imagine we're back at home in the kitchen:

We forgot the ketchup!

Don't worry. I've got a few sachets in my bumbag.

I thought you said they were bite-size! I'll never manage a full one.

Oh! This fish just melts in your mouth.

Wish I'd worn my elasticated trousers.

But I don't close my eyes. I'm watching Daniel. I've left his tray open on his lap, trying to tease him with the smell and the heat. *Stimulate his senses.*

So far it's not working. His body is rigid, knuckles white as he presses his hands into his face, squishing his nose down.

Daniel and Chipz

– Nnnnggghh, I say.

– Stay strong, buddy. Stay strong, whispers Chipz in my ear.

And I WANT to stay strong. I WANT to do what Chipz tells me, but the SMELL is still there and I REALLY LIKE IT and I can't help myself and I move my fingers an EENY-WEENY BIT to let a little more of the SMELL into my SCHNOZZ.

Megan

Dad's trying to drive one-handed. The windscreen's misted up so he puts the blowers on hot.

'What are you doing?' snaps Grandma. 'It's stuffy enough already. I'll keel over at this rate.'

'I can't see where I'm going,' says Dad. 'I'll end up crashing into a hippo, and then we'll be done for.'

'Pssshh,' says Grandma, pushing down the electric window. Refreshing cool air fills the car.

Dad waves his wooden fork towards a sign.

KEEP WINDOWS
CLOSED
AT ALL TIMES

Grandma wheezes dramatically. 'But I need the fresh air. I've got a twisted lung.'

'Rules are rules,' says Mum.

Grandma glares at her then squeezes out an almighty fart.

'Ah, gross,' I say. The grim stench fights against the lovely smell of the chips.

'Crikey! Did someone step on a duck?' says Dad.

'Not my fault,' says Grandma. 'I warned you. Twisted lung. The air's got to escape somehow. And if you won't let me ventilate myself then ...'

'Fine,' croaks Mum, holding her nose. 'Leave it open just a crack.'

I turn back to Daniel. In the old days, Grandma squeezing cheese would've made him laugh till he turned blue. Today, of course, it doesn't register.

But hang on. Is it me or have his hands moved a little bit? I swear I couldn't see his mouth and nose a minute ago.

'Come on,' I say to him. 'You must be starving. You eat other food. Why not your favourite? Here. Try a chip.'

I stab one with my fork and hold it towards his mouth. It's thick and caramel-coloured. A couple of salt crystals glisten on the surface, suspended in a little bubble of vinegar.

His nose twitches.

I can tell he's seriously tempted. He gulps and his throat quivers. His nostrils flare.

Then he nudges my arm away with Monkey.

Daniel and Chipz

— Get outta here! says Chipz all shouty, and he

does his special kung-fu karate moves on the person holding the chip.

Then he notices me sniffing. Hey! Whatcha doin', man? he says, all snappy.

— Er . . . er . . . nothing, I say and now I feel SUPER-TURQUOISE GUILTY, because I was trying my best not to smell the smell but I couldn't HELP IT.

— You're drooling!

— No, I'm not.

— You are. You're drooling like a freakin' dog. Quit it already! Jeez.

And I screw my face up even tighter and I try. I really, REALLY TRY.

Megan

I'm not giving up that easily.

He pushes me away again with Monkey, less forcefully this time. Then his tongue darts out across his moist lips. He jiggles Monkey in front of his face and screws up his eyes.

Why is he fighting it? Why won't he just take the chip, for God's sake?

Maybe I should try something.

Quick as I can, I grab the hand with Monkey in it and pin it to his thigh. Daniel clamps his mouth shut but, using my other hand, I gently stroke the chip across his lips. At first he squirms and resists, but soon he relaxes, like he *wants* me to overpower him. 'Here. Just try one. They're delicious.'

'What's going on?' says Dad.

Mum tries to pull on my shoulder. 'Megan. I'm not sure ab—'

'Pinch his nose together so he can't breathe. S'what we did in the olden days,' says Grandma, a little too cheerfully.

I'm not going *that* far. 'Just take a nibble . . .' I say, as his lips slowly ease apart. 'I know you want to.'

Daniel and Chipz

— Don't. Eat. It, Monkey says, panting and straining like he can't breathe.

And I don't want to eat it but I DO want to eat it. And the chip smells SOOOO GOOD and I can feel the warmth on my knees, and the fat and the stingy vinegar on my lips and it's making my tummy grumble like CRAZY and before I know it my mouth is open and the chip is INSIDE and a FIREWORK OF FLAVOUR goes off on my tongue and it's a

GAZLLION times better than yesterday's chip —
CRISPY on the outside and SOFT and FLUFFY on
the inside — and now I'm swallowing it and I want
more and Chipz is moaning all muffly and I'm sorry,
Chipz. I'm sorry but now there are four in my mouth
ALL AT ONCE and they're so TASTY and I have the
white even though there is also the Turquoise
which is guilt but I cannot HELP IT and I am so
sorry Chipz.

My mouth is stuffed and the white is
everywhere and I greedily grab more with my
fingers and then I see them.

FACES.

I stop chewing even though my cheeks are full of
chips.

Isn't that STRANGE?!

I feel like I'm seeing the faces for the FIRST
TIME but maybe also NOT for the FIRST TIME. They
look NEW but also NOT NEW.

Girl brown hair.

Man hair brown a little bit grey and a hairy
chin.

Woman brown hair.

Really old woman with crinkly old face and white
hair.

How PECULIAR!

I don't get it. Had I not NOTICED their faces before now or had I just not SEEN them at all? I'd never noticed NOT noticing them, I don't think. I try to imagine what I saw BEFORE NOW when I looked at the people's faces, but I can't get a picture in my head and it gives me a BRAIN PAIN.

I feel like telling Monkey, but part of me thinks this would be a BAD IDEA.

And they all smile at me apart from the REALLY OLD WOMAN who has gone back to eating her chips so I can only see the back of her head.

So I smile back at them and they smile even more and the white feeling is actually taking over and

THREE HOURS LATER

Megan

We're in a hotel room at a service station. I say *room* – it's more just a dingy white box that smells like unwashed bobble hats, with a constant *ZHUM ZHUM ZHUM* from the motorway in the background.

'At least it's clean,' said Dad when we got here.

Yech. Clean like a fresh coffin.

It's got a TV, but there's no on-demand and the Wi-Fi doesn't work, so we're stuck with whatever's on. At 4 p.m. that limits us to kids' programmes, or gameshows for the nearly-dead.

I switch the TV off and flump back onto the bed I'll be sharing with Daniel tonight. He's over as far as he can go, jammed up against the wall with Monkey clutched in his arms and his fingers pinched over his nose.

4 p.m.! Jeez. What are we going to do in this little prison cell between now and bedtime?

ZHUM. ZHUM. ZHUM.

There are pictures on the wall: horrible things – just

splodges of different-coloured paint, splashed and scraped and dolloped all over the place. They're absolutely rubbish, like a puppy's crashed through a school paint cupboard then rolled across a piece of paper. I blur my eyes to see if this makes them any better. It doesn't. I stand up and walk up and down the narrow space between our bed and Mum and Dad's double.

'What are you doing?' asks Mum, without looking up.

'Just going for a hike,' I grumble. 'Spot of sightseeing.'

No response.

For the last twenty minutes, Mum's been hunched over the desk, which has a built-in bottle opener so people don't open beer bottles against the desktop. From all the gouges and scratches on the wood, I'm guessing they still do.

When we first got here, she spent ages trying to engage with Daniel. She's decided that Dad's 'chip experiment' has failed miserably so it's time for her to take over. She tried all these different things she'd read about in one of her books – putting a pen and paper on the pillow next to him and asking him to draw a picture of his feelings; telling him a story about a monkey who had an accident and asking him what the monkey should do next; putting a bag of Lego next to him and asking to build something for her.

Of course he didn't pay her any attention, and now she's furiously jotting down a list of things she'll need to pack for him when he goes to stay at the clinic.

It's all gone wrong.

ZHUM. ZHUM. ZHUM.

Bored. Bored. Bored.

Sad. Sad. Sad.

Things were going *brilliantly* too – the way Daniel ate the chips. The way he looked at us. The way his eyes opened wide like he was actually *seeing* us. And then . . .

I slump back down on the bed.

I should've gone next door to the service station with Dad to find something for tea. I begged him to get us a KFC but Mum said she didn't want anything with chips after what happened this afternoon. Dad said he'd see what they had in Waitrose.

ZHUM. ZHUM. ZHUM. ZHUM.

There's a Bible by the bed. I open it. On the first page someone's written: 'And on the eighth day, God stayed in this crummy hole and gave up on life.'

ZHUM. ZHUM.

I can't even talk to Grandma to distract myself.

She was so upset after what happened at the safari park that she demanded a separate room.

I decide to boil the kettle, just for something to do.

And we were so close as well.

So there we were, in the safari park.

Daniel was looking at us – and I mean *really* looking at us. For the first time since the accident, he actually seemed like he knew we were there. Like he knew *who we were*. His mouth dropped open, half-chewed chips slopping all over his tongue. OK – it *was* disgusting. But it was also amazing – he was like an explorer who'd just opened a tomb full of jewels.

The whole world seemed to stop.

I felt like I could cry. My fingers dug into Monkey on the side of Daniel's leg.

And this big wave of understanding washed over me.

How could we have been so dumb?

Ever since the accident, Daniel has needed Monkey. Obsessed about it. Taken it everywhere. Never even let it out of his hands for a second – in the bath, on the loo, you name it.

Like the doctor said: *Monkey acts as a barrier, a shield.*

And that's what we've known all along. So we've just thought: *Monkey is a barrier. It protects him from the world. Don't take it off him because then he gets upset and he feels unsafe.*

But barriers work two ways.

So yeah, sure, Monkey *might* be protecting Daniel. It *might* be helping him feel safe while he's trapped inside his own head, frightened of the real world after his accident.

But maybe that's not it.

Maybe *Monkey* is what's trapping him? Maybe he'd feel safer and be more happy if we could get Monkey off him for good? I mean, here he was, Monkey pinned to his leg, big hamster cheeks full of mushed-up chips, and for the first time in ages he was *recognising us.*

Maybe, all along, this was all we had to do.

Ditch Monkey; replace it quickly with some other things he liked. Maybe then he'd be OK. Maybe then we'd *all* be OK.

So I did it. I carried on stuffing chips into his mouth, while slowly, slowly easing Monkey out of his hand.

'Nyep. Nyep,' he said, grinning and chewing, not noticing Monkey gradually moving from his grip.

His hand relaxed as Monkey slid past his palm and into his fingers.

My heart pounded right up to my throat.

Just a few more centimetres.

But then it all went wrong.

'Wow,' said Dad flatly. 'Would you look at that!'

I froze. Monkey was now only loosely held in Daniel's fingertips, his eyes blissfully closed as he chewed.

Dad was pointing ahead of us at a battered hatchback.

It had a car sticker in the back that said 'Little Princess on Board'. A toddler – I guess she was standing on someone's knee – was leaning right out of the passenger window. She had a doughnut in her hand and was offering it to a giraffe, even though that's like the dumbest thing I've ever seen.

The giraffe was loving it – spreading its legs and bending its neck down and slurping the doughnut with its huge tongue. But then the toddler suddenly started wailing and dropped the doughnut. The giraffe ate it up off the ground and the toddler was yanked back inside the window.

Just before the car sped up, someone shoved their arm out the passenger window and gave the giraffe the middle finger.

I'm serious. The middle finger. What kind of person does that to a freaking giraffe?

I was so gobsmacked that, for just a few seconds, I forgot what I was trying to do with Monkey. If only the person in front wasn't such an idiot. If only I'd just pulled Monkey away right then when I had the chance.

But I didn't. I hesitated. And this was a massive mistake.

Look, I'm not saying that the giraffe was annoyed about being given the finger. I think it was probably just excited about the doughnut and wanted to know what treats *we* had.

Whatever.

The thing is, as soon as we rolled up to it, its pointy

head nuzzled the side of our car. Then its tongue emerged.

It was *disgusting*: this big long purply-black snake of a thing, slurping across Grandma's window, leaving a long streak of slimy drool across the glass. The window was still half open though, so then the tongue flapped *inside* the car.

Horrible.

It twisted in through the gap like a bendy arm, reaching round and flicking right across Grandma's hair.

'Aaaargh!' she squawked.

'Shut the window!' cried Mum.

But Grandma was flapping about so much that she ended up jabbing the wrong button and the window went *down* instead of up, and before we knew it the whole of the giraffe's massive head was bumping about *inside* the car. Grandma was pushing it away and yelling at it to get its stinky face out of here, and the giraffe looked right at me and Daniel and curled its lips up into this weird toothy leer and Daniel just cracked up, laughing and clapping like this was the funniest thing ever.

It was so nice seeing him like that, so beautiful.

But it didn't last long.

The giraffe knocked Grandma's tray, scattering chips all over her front. Its tongue emerged again and coiled inside her top, guzzling the chips off her chest.

'Help!' she squawked.

Dad tried to push the giraffe's head off Grandma, but it wouldn't budge. 'His tongue's in my bra, the dirty beast!' she screamed.

The next thing, she's punching it in the face.

Yes! That's right. My grandma was PUNCHING a GIRAFFE IN THE FLIPPING FACE and Mum was ordering Dad to 'DRIVE!' but Dad was shouting that he couldn't drive because there was a giraffe in the car, and in any case Grandma was sprawled sideways across him, her body covering the gear stick, with the giraffe's tongue slobbering all over her and gobbling up the chips off her wrinkly old knockers.

It was total chaos.

I glanced at Daniel, who was laughing so much that bits of chewed-up chip were spraying out of his mouth.

And that's when I remembered about Monkey.

I glanced at the window. At the giraffe. At Daniel. Everyone's minds were on other things. The perfect moment. I yanked Monkey out of his hand, leaned forward and chucked it past the giraffe's head and out of the window.

Daniel howled.

This wasn't what I'd expected. And it clearly wasn't what the giraffe expected either. Terrified, it thrashed its head around, bonking its horns on the ceiling as it struggled to escape.

At that moment, three zebra-striped Land Rovers came bumping across the grass towards us from different directions, and the giraffe pulled its head out and galloped away.

Twenty seconds later, six park rangers were standing by the car.

They found Grandma half-dressed and draped across her seat with chips and giraffe spit all over her, Daniel screeching and headbutting the windows and practically snapping off the door handle, and a tailless cuddly toy and a half-eaten doughnut lying on the ground by the car.

One of the rangers handed the toy back through the window. 'I think maybe we should escort you to the exit,' she said.

Daniel reached forward, snatched Monkey out of her hand and buried himself back under his duffel coat.

Daniel and Chipz

We are lying on a bed together, pressed up against the wall. I don't like the smell of the bed because it is NOT the smell of MY BED so I am cuddling Chipz REALLY TIGHT. But Chipz isn't cuddling me back.

It was awful when Chipz flew out of the window like that. ANYTHING could've happened to him. I wanted to ESCAPE and RESCUE him, but the giraffe was there and the door wouldn't open and the Red came so bad it was almost Black and maybe I hit things but I don't know and in the end somebody handed him back in through the window and I hugged him TIGHT with my eyes closed so that I did not have to look at those faces and I did not open my eyes again until we got here into this room.

— I feel Turquoise, I say.

— Nah. Ya don't need to be guilty, he says in a HAPPY way that shows me he is NOT MAD, which is a RELIEF. But then his face goes serious and he says all growly, Just promise me you'll never, EVER pull a stunt like that again.

I gulp because I am scared and the Orange comes again. Promise, I say, all weak and soft.

And even though I am scared, I know he is right. I should NOT have eaten those chips and I should NOT have smiled at those faces and I should NOT have laughed at the funny giraffe. I forgot Chipz was there, which was UNACCEPTABLE, because it meant that the girl threw him out of the window.

— We're meant to be a team, he says.

– I know, I say SUPER-SADLY.

He nods his head which is a kind look, and he says, Look. Forget about it. Ya know what? I wanna change my name back to Monkey. I hate Chipz.

This makes me a tiny bit HAPPIER. I prefer the name Monkey. And things were getting too CONFUSING when he was called Chipz.

– Shall we play something? I ask because I want to DISTRACT myself from Monkey being mad and from the SMELL of the BED and from OTHER THINGS that are bothering me.

And Monkey says, Yeah, man. Let's get under the covers. We can pretend we're exploring underground caves. Miles away from anyone else.

I am HAPPY to do this but I also feel NOT GOOD. I have a really, REALLY bad secret I cannot tell him about which is this: I feel really Turquoise guilty about eating the chips and smiling at those faces NOW, but I did NOT feel bad AT THE TIME, even when Monkey was being squashed. It was only when he flew out of the window that I started to feel bad and I DON'T UNDERSTAND WHY.

In fact, seeing those faces felt really nice, like a little white fire warming me up inside.

Megan

The kettle has just boiled (it took four minutes and eleven seconds, and the fact I timed it shows exactly how bored and down I'm feeling) when Dad comes back in, looking amazingly cheerful. He kisses Mum on the head and drops the shopping bags onto the bed. She doesn't look up.

Daniel's feet are poking out from under the covers of the other bed, so who knows what he's up to? As long as his gross socks don't touch my pillow, it's all right.

He calmed down a bit after he got Monkey back, but he hasn't looked at any of us since. It's so frustrating. It felt like he was back with us just for those few moments. If only the giraffe hadn't shoved its head in. If only I'd got rid of Monkey slowly instead of snatching it away.

If only that car hadn't smashed into him in the first place.

'This is fun, isn't it?' Dad says to me. 'Hotel. Picnic in the bedroom.'

I push my hair out of my eyes and tilt my head at him as if to say, *Are you nuts?!*

He doesn't notice. 'Oh, has the kettle just boiled? Lovely. Tea, please, Meg. I bought proper milk.'

I make one for him and one for Mum, using the

individually wrapped teabags. It's something to do. Mum still doesn't look up.

'Look,' says Dad to both of us, 'I know this isn't perfect, but let's look on the bright side. Daniel spoke real words again. And holy Moses – I will never, ever forget Grandma smacking a giraffe in the chops.'

I half laugh. I mean, it *was* pretty funny.

Dad continues. 'Getting chucked out of the safari park was a hoot too. Bit like the old days, eh, Karen? Remember when you got arrested on that protest march?'

Mum's shoots him a *not in front of Megan* face.

Wow! Mum got arrested! How cool is that?! I mean, I knew she used to be a bit of a punk, but I've only ever seen photos.

'Tell me more,' I say, desperate for something exciting.

'No,' says Mum.

'Well,' says Dad, ignoring her, 'it was our first date – the week after she'd stolen that chip. I said, *Let's do something together?* Thinking maybe I could take her to the cinema or something, but she says, *Ten thousand of us are marching to 10 Downing Street, because we don't like loud bangs.*'

Mum huffs. 'Nuclear missiles. We wanted the government to get rid of its nuclear missiles, as well you know. And I'd rather not talk about it.'

Dad doesn't seem to notice. 'Whatever. So we're marching along and there's this policeman at the side of the road, bending over to tie his laces, and she just runs up behind him and kicks him up the b—'

'I said STOP with the stories and grow up!' snaps Mum, slamming her pen down.

'What do you mean, stories?' asks Dad eventually. His voice is croaky.

'You're always telling stories. *Remember when you kicked that policeman. Remember when we met at that chip van.* I'm sick of it.'

Dad looks hurt. 'But I like to remember . . .'

'It's not just the stories,' she says. 'Everything's got to be a big laugh to you. We've got things to worry about and you're dragging us round the country to find fish and chips.'

'Bu—'

'Look. I'll let you do your ridiculous Chip Shop Challenge because I know it's important to you. But then we're going home and we're doing the proper, grown-up thing and sending Daniel to that clinic. And that is that.'

She turns back to her scribblings.

The room is silent for what seems like ages.

'I do have a reason for going to these chip shops, you know,' says Dad quietly.

'Are you going to tell me what it is?' sighs Mum.

'No. Like I said, it's a surprise. And I've decided – I don't care what happens. We're not going home till we've done them all.'

Mum shakes her head and laughs without any joy at all.
'Please yourself.'

Daniel and Monkey

Monkey and I crawl under the covers together,
and we find ourselves in a tiny, tight CAVE with
cold, wet walls and STALAGMITES which grow up
with all their might and STALACTITES which come
down like a lady's tights, which is a funny joke I
heard once but I don't remember who said it. We
are wearing dirty orange OVERALLS and helmets
with lights on the front, and the cave is just
about wide enough for us to crawl down together.

Or at least I really, REALLY want to think that
I'm in a cave, but actually I know that it's all just
PRETEND. Actually we're under the covers of a BED
and the walls are just SHEETS that smell a BIT
FUSTY and the stalactites are just crumply bits of
BLANKET.

Your Guide to the Best Fish and Chip Shops in the UK

3) Asquith's Traditional Fish and Chip Shop, Yorkshire

Established over eighty years ago, Asquith's is nestled in the beautiful Yorkshire Dales National Park. Busloads of tourists flock to its sit-down restaurant, and this family-run business is right at the heart of the local community – delivering food to remote, rural areas and organising a whole host of village events.

Megan

We're on the motorway. The next chippy is 183 miles away, according to the route Dad sent to my phone – right back up the middle of the country and into a big green patch on the map. It's actually not far from our house, so it seems like a really long round trip just for some grub.

After what happened at the safari park yesterday, today is officially Suck Up to Grandma Day. She's still in a stinking mood.

First thing in the morning, Dad went to the service station and brought her back a bag of M&M's, a newspaper, and a hot chocolate and a pastry from Starbucks. He left them on the floor outside her room then knocked on the door and scampered off down the corridor.

I wish I'd been bitten by a giraffe. I had to make do with a variety pack of Frosties with a tiny warm splash of last night's leftover milk.

We all trooped back round to collect her about an hour later.

When she opened her door, Dad beamed at her. 'How did you sleep?'

'Rubbish,' grumbled Grandma. 'Trust you to book us into somewhere cheap. Mattress was about as comfortable as a glass-juggler's bin bag. I need Memory Foam with my ingrowing bones.'

What the hell are ingrowing bones?

Dad tried to speak but she cut him off. 'And before you ask, no, I was not impressed by your pathetic attempts to apologise. Hot chocolate – cold and sickly. Newspaper – crumpled. Croissants – can't stand 'em. And Peanut M&M's? With my false teeth? Did you fall out of the stupid tree this morning?'

Before I could mention that she'd bought herself Peanut M&M's two days ago, she'd already swept past, her stick going *kajunk-kajunk-kajunk* down the corridor.

I went into her room to get her suitcase. The hot chocolate cup – empty, with her pink lipstick marks round the top – was in the bin, as were the wrapper for the croissant and the empty M&M's bag. The disgusting sucked-clean peanuts from inside the M and Ms stood in a row on the desk like gravestones for dead mice. The newspaper was open at the crossword (completed).

I chuckled to myself.

She's a stubborn old bird.

'Right then,' says Dad as we bomb along. 'How about we give scores out of ten for yesterday's chip shop?'

He's still acting jolly, as if he didn't have that big row with Mum yesterday. This is him all over – trying to look on the bright side of everything. Meanwhile Mum's barely spoken since we got up.

'Megan,' he says, rummaging in the storage compartment under the gear stick and then handing me back Daniel's notebook, 'you write them down.'

It seems like the right thing to do. I take it off him and find a pen in my school rucksack, which is still on the floor by my feet.

'Minus five,' says Grandma. 'They must've sprinkled giraffe bait on mine.'

Dad sniggers.

'Breaking and entering into a lady's brassiere is not a laughing matter,' she snaps. 'Whether it's perpetrated by man or giraffe. As soon as we get home I shall write to the safari park and demand that they have the animal put down.'

'Quite right,' says Dad, eyes twinkling at me in the rear-view mirror. 'Once they've got a taste for underwear, they'll never stop. Knickers next. Then boxers. Before you know it they'll be trampling people to death for their thongs.'

I laugh into my hand.

'That's the first sensible thing you've said today,' says Grandma stiffly, the joke sailing over her head. 'I'd wring the dirty beggar's neck myself if someone would hold the stepladder. Make it a minus ten actually.'

'Very generous of you too. I'll give it an eight,' Dad says. 'Karen?'

'What?' says Mum, looking up from her work iPad. She's been finding out everything she can about that clinic since we left the hotel an hour ago.

'Scores out of ten.'

'What for?'

'Yesterday's chippy.'

'Oh. Right. Whatever. Seven? What's it for?'

Trying not to get cross, I jot it down. Nine from me. I glance over at Daniel. I reckon he'd say nine too – he enjoyed the ones he had. So that makes . . . 'Twenty-three out of fifty.'

I think that's a bit harsh – even though it ended in a disaster, their chips *were* delicious. For a moment I think about ignoring Grandma's score, but then I decide not to. I want to do it properly.

'Seen the scores, Snotface?' I ask Daniel, but he ignores me, frowning and staring at the floor.

'Would you like to look at the route?' I say, putting the notebook on my knee and holding my phone in front of his eyes. 'Here. See it?'

His face remains blank.

I wish I could tell if he can hear me or not.

Daniel and Monkey

I am in the car with the people again. It's strange though. I can't recognise their faces today. Monkey said this is a GOOD THING because I shouldn't be FRATERNISING with TERRORISTS. I think he is a bit RIGHT about this even though I don't know what fraternising means.

But he is also A BIT WRONG, because I had a THINK when I woke up in the middle of the night which was that MAYBE they are NOT TOTALLY BAD because they gave me CHIPS yesterday and they made me feel white, so that means they aren't TERRORISTS, which are people with BOMBS up their JUMPERS.

One of the people who sounded maybe like the girl was speaking to me just now. WAARK WAARK WAARK. Part of me wanted to look at her but I didn't because I promised Monkey and he always says that a BEST PAL'S PROMISE should never be BROKE.

— Hey yo, D-Namite. I been thinkin', says Monkey.

— What about? I say.

— We should DEFINITELY run away together, he says.

— You mean like when we go to SEA or SPACE or into a CAVE? I say.

— No. I mean we need to get away. Forever. Before it's too late. Things are gettin' real nasty, man.

I'm feeling a mood I don't really know. I wish I had a colour for it. Maybe it's a CREAM mood or something — it's like when you know something is strange and wrong and you are worried like Orange, but you don't know WHAT you're worried about and you can't say anything to your best friend about it so it builds up really quickly. It makes my head hurt, so I press it against the glass and I make my nnnngggghhh sound.

— Hey, hey, hey, relax, man, relax, says Monkey.

And I stop making my noise and I feel CALMER again and Monkey says, This is why we gotta get outta here, man. It's stressin' you out. But don't worry about it today. Take your time to think about it. You got your best pal lookin' out for ya.

And I take some DEEP BREATHS and calm down and I say, Thank you, Monkey.

But actually it was NOT Monkey who calmed me down. It was SOMETHING I've just seen on the FLOOR that I know I can't tell him about.

— You OK? he says.

146

And I say yes.

But I know I don't want to run away.

I don't want to go away from those people I saw yesterday – the man, the woman, the girl, the old woman. They gave me a NICE FEELING when I saw their faces and I think that if I stay here I might see them AGAIN.

And also I don't want to run away because of the SOMETHING I've just seen on the floor which is what reminded me of the nice white feeling I got from the people yesterday, and gave me another nice feeling on top.

Megan

We've been stuck in this traffic jam for *ages*.

Grandma's cheered up a bit. She found a two-day-old cheese roll in her bumbag and she's pulled out her false teeth so she can suck it till it disintegrates. Utterly disgusting.

Mum's on her phone, still finding out about this clinic – who the doctors are, what treatments they offer. Occasionally she'll say something like, 'D'you know, there's a garden there for walking in, and even a croquet pitch?' or

'Can you believe Professor Spielman is in charge? You know – the one who wrote that book I was telling you about.'

Dad makes half-interested grunting noises, but seems to be more interested in the terrible music on the radio.

My phone's just died – Mum unplugged it last night when I was asleep because hers *needed charging* and *Dad didn't think to pack her charger.*

Great.

I can't even look at the map to watch our blue dot not moving.

At least Daniel's calmed down. He's silently staring at the floor and has been for ages.

A while ago he got really worked up, started making all these noises and bashing his head against the window. On the one hand, this was horrible – I hate seeing him upset, and you always worry that he's going to hurt himself.

But now I think about it, it gives me a tiny spark of hope: is it a sign he's getting a little bit better? I mean, he's hardly had any flip-outs since the accident, except when he thinks people are getting too close to Monkey. Now he's had – *what?* – two or three in the last few days. And I've just remembered – last night he held his nose in bed, as if he didn't like the smell in the room. That hasn't happened since he got run over either. Unfamiliar smells used to really bother him, but they just don't any more.

It makes me realise: if we ever *do* get Daniel back, we'll

have to put up with the *whole Daniel,* good and bad. But I'd take that any day of the week.

I glance over at him. 'Fancy a game of Car Bingo, Snotface?'

Before the accident, we never got bored in the car. Boredom was bad news for Daniel – the first step towards a wig-out – so we always had to keep him distracted. Car Bingo was our favourite game – I'd take red, black and grey and he'd have white, yellow and blue. You'd get a point for each one that you saw. First person to spot a pink would get ten bonus points. The winner was the first to a hundred. I'd always pretend not to see my cars so I could let him win. I had a massive advantage because my colours were way more popular than his, but those colours made him think of bad moods so he would never choose them.

Daniel doesn't reply to me. The tiny spark of hope fades away. Who was I trying to kid?

The cars in the next lane start moving, but for a second I'm not sure if it's them going forward or us going backwards. Then we set off at the same speed as them, and it's hard to tell if both lanes are moving forward or we're both standing still.

Ms Cocker, my English teacher, would say there's a metaphor in there somewhere.

She'd probably be right.

What happens if we go to all five chip shops and nothing

changes? What if yesterday was as good as it gets? I don't want to think about Daniel going away to this clinic. But I don't want to think of him being like this forever either. And what if our family never gets fixed?

I rub my eyes.

Then I take out Daniel's notebook and draw two tables – one for his colours of cars, one for mine – and I tick them off until the tears are so heavy on my eyelashes that the cars are just coloured blobs.

Daniel

I try not to think about THE THING ON THE FLOOR but it keeps coming into my head. It's like this game I once played with a lady, when the lady said, Try not to think about a PINK ELEPHANT! And we laughed so much because you can't stop thinking about a pink elephant when someone says DON'T and suddenly I am thinking about the BOAT we bashed into when we were pirates.

And that makes me think: WERE we ACTUALLY pirates or were we just PRETENDING to be pirates?

— Sure you're OK? says Monkey.

And I blink three times and say, yes, very quickly.

But the THING ON THE FLOOR is REALLY IN MY
BRAIN and I've GOT to do something or I'm going to
go CRACKER-WHACKER-DING-DONG.

So I take a BIG GULP to gulp away the Turquoise
and I say, Hey, Monkey, would you like to play a
GAME?

— Sure, he says.

— How about a WHO CAN GO TO SLEEP FIRST
game? I say, and I try to keep my voice normal.

— A what? says Monkey and he looks at me over
his sunglasses all suspicious.

— The winner is the one who falls asleep fi—

But Monkey's already face down on my lap going
honk-shoo-ooh-ah-ah.

— Oh you CHEEKY SNEAK! I say, because he
cheated by asking me a question to distract me
and now he is the winner.

But actually I am HAPPY he did this. And actually
THIS was my TOP-SECRET plan all along. Shhhhh.
Very gently, I lift his arm to see if he really is
asleep. It flops down onto my leg.

I'd better do this DOUBLE-QUICK-FAST.

Megan

I don't want anyone to see me crying so I turn away from Mum even though she's not paying me any attention anyway. And that's when I look at Daniel.

Monkey's lying face down across his lap. Daniel carefully lifts its hand up and drops it down again. His teeth are gritted and he slowly lets out his seat belt and bends forward towards the floor.

'What are you do—' I ask him.

He freezes and stares at me, wide-eyed with fear. And for one tiny second there's this little connection between us and I *know* he wants me to keep quiet, so I put my finger over my lips.

Then Daniel does the same.

Oh my word.

He copied me!

I feel like properly sobbing but I have to hold it in, terrified of breaking the spell.

Daniel leans down to the floor, snatches up a day-old chip off the carpet and shoves it into his gob.

It kind of ruins the moment.

'Snotface! That is gross!' I say.

Everyone looks at him.

Alarmed, Daniel spins towards the window to chew and swallow the chip. Then he turns back and opens his mouth to Monkey.

Disgusting.

Daniel and Monkey

WAARK WAARK SNOTFACE WAARK.

Monkey sits up straight and says, Hey, yo. Did I win?

And I feel REALLY Turquoise as I say, Yes. Yes, you won. Well done, Monkey!

And he looks at me all squinty and says, Hey — you OK, Big D?

And I show him my mouth and say, I'm not eating anything, Monkey, honest.

— Hmmm, says Monkey, like maybe he does NOT BELIEVE me, and now I think I shouldn't have SHOWN him my mouth because that maybe made it look like I HAD been eating something and that I was feeling Turquoise GUILTY about it.

He doesn't say anything for a while so I say, Should we go into the jungle, where there's nobody but us? Or the desert maybe?

And Monkey takes a big, long, deep breath. Then he SMILES and says, Sure thing, DJ D-Funk. Let's go to the desert. We can catch us some SNAKES.

And he says the word snakes just a little bit LOUD, and I'm not sure why but I try not to think about it because I feel big RELIEF which is actually almost a white feeling like a flower opening up. And I pick my teeth because there is still a little bit of chip in there and even though it was a bit SOGGY and RUBBERY and CARPETY, I could still taste the salty, vinegary CHIPPINESS of it and it makes my tummy ache for more.

And there was something else nice, which was SEEING the girl's face again, even for just a SECOND.

Megan

We're here and it's very nice, I guess; a little village in a valley – all narrow lanes and dry stone walls. It looks like something out of *Postman Pat*. When Daniel was little, Dad used to dress up as Mrs Goggins and he and Daniel would spend hours weighing pretend parcels in the kitchen.

It's now past three o'clock. We've had a proper mission

getting here – roadworks, escaped sheep, traffic jams, the lot. Apart from Grandma – and Daniel with his solitary floor chip – we haven't eaten since breakfast. I'm starving.

At least we're here now.

And, despite everything, we're all quite cheerful.

I've been a bit happier ever since Daniel looked at me. He *saw* me again. I know he did. Dad and Grandma are excited about the food, and Mum's pleased because we're half an hour from home and *we could end this preposterous trip right now if we wanted to*.

We park up, climb out and have a stretch. I make sure I grab my charger. There might be somewhere to plug my phone in.

'Five minutes and we'll be gobbling down a plateful of fish and chips,' says Dad, rubbing his hands together. 'I'm going for a large, I think. With mushy peas. And thick gravy.'

Mmmmm. Gravy.

We head over to the chip shop, which dominates the high street of the little village. It's an enormous grey stone building, set over a couple of floors. Just the sight of it makes my mouth water. There are two front doors – one for the restaurant and one for the take-away counter, which seems to be closed. Four or five minibuses are parked outside, all from places like Golden Sunset Retirement Home and The Staying Alive Over Seventies Club.

'Must be a favourite with the oldies,' says Dad.

We reach the chippy. In the glass front door, surrounded by Good Food Award stickers, I can see the same newspaper cut-out that Daniel has in his notebook. The entry for this place is highlighted pink. It seems like everywhere that's mentioned on the list likes to make a big deal out of it.

We open the door and make our way upstairs.

Daniel and Monkey

In the car, Monkey seemed a lot happier once we went to the desert. We went hunting for SCORPIONS and RATTLESNAKES and then we had an imaginary sand-ball fight.

— Great shot, man! You got sand in my butt! said Monkey.

— Oh no! I hope I didn't hurt your TERRIBLE INJURY! I said.

— Course not, buddy! He laughed.

I laughed too, but actually I knew that the sand couldn't really hurt the hole where his TAIL used to be because the SAND was PRETEND. This is because we weren't REALLY in a DESERT, we were ACTUALLY in a Citroën Grand Picasso, and we weren't ON OUR OWN because those other people were in there with us and the whole thing was IMAGINARY.

Then the car stopped and we got out and we could stop pretending, and actually this felt like a RELIEF, like when you hold your wee in because you are OUT AND ABOUT and you don't like using public toilets due to the GERMS and the STINK but then you finally get home to your FAVOURITE toilet just before you WET YOURSELF. And isn't that funny? Because I don't know when I've ever used a public toilet or what one is.

We are outside a building.

— I love escaping with you, man. You're the best pal a monkey could wish for, says Monkey.

And I gulp because suddenly the TURQUOISE comes back and it is like a thick rope STRANGLING me. This time I feel GUILTY because Monkey doesn't know that I was only IMAGINING in the car, not going to the desert in REAL LIFE. Plus I'm still guilty about the CHIP I ate from the FLOOR. And maybe I'm NOT the BEST PAL A MONKEY COULD WISH FOR.

So I say, Sorry, Monkey.

And he looks at me funny and says, Sorry for what?

And I don't know what to say so I splutter for a

bit then I say, Er . . . sorry I wasn't there when you had your TERRIBLE ACCIDENT.

– Don't sweat it. You're here for me now. And you'll be here for me forever, right? says Monkey.

But I don't answer this because now there's YET ANOTHER thing to be sorry for. Another reason for the TURQUOISE ROPE to get TIGHTER round my NECK.

I can smell chips.

And they smell absolutely AMAZ-A-DINGA-DING-DONG-DELICIOUS.

Megan

We go up the stairs and through an open doorway into the restaurant.

Whoa!

I wasn't expecting this. The place is completely rammed.

I'd guess there are two hundred people in here. Most are sitting down to eat at tables. A few more are on a kind of dance-floor area in the corner of the room. They're hobbling around in pairs to painfully slow jazz music. The music is being played by a trio of fossilised musicians who look like they might actually die at any moment.

It takes me a while to realise something about the people: every single one of them is a white-haired, crinkly old codger. They all look like they've stepped out of a Werther's Originals advert.

Seriously, I don't think I've ever been in a room with so many old people before. Their average age must be about a hundred and ninety-three. In fact, apart from the staff, the only non-wrinklies are a tableful of nurses, huddled in the corner as far away from everyone else as possible.

A waitress hurries past to the kitchen hatch without looking at us.

'Two sausage and chips and a special for table three,' she says, shoving a slip of paper through the gap. In the kitchen, I can see three sweaty men slaving away at deep-fat fryers.

One of them comes to the hatch and slides two plates out onto the counter. 'Service. Two fish specials for table eight.'

'They're in a proper bad mood this week,' says the waitress, snatching up the plates and turning back. 'Someone must've let the tyres down on their wheelchairs or summat.'

Dad steps in front of her. She stops abruptly, one painted eyebrow raised like an angry black rainbow.

The plates are balanced in her hands, inches from my face. The fish is enormous and thick and curly, nestled on a golden-brown mountain of chips. Bright green mushy peas hug the edge of the plates. I have to stop myself from diving face first into them.

Dad clears his throat. 'Table for f—'

The girl tuts at him. 'Can you not read?'

She nods to a poster on the door behind us. We hadn't seen it because the door was open.

SORRY!
RESTAURANT CLOSED 2—6.
MONTHLY PENSIONERS'
TEA DANCE AND CHIP SUPPER

Closed again!

This is becoming a habit.

'By gum, you useless clot,' Grandma says to Dad. 'You couldn't rustle up a fart after a baked-bean dinner.'

'How was I supposed to know?' says Dad.

'You want chips, you need a ticket,' says the girl, blowing her fringe out of her eyes. She tries to sidestep Dad but he won't let her go.

'And where do I . . . ?' he asks.

'At the desk over there, or –' she scans him head to toe – 'from your old people's home.'

Ouch.

She struts off through the room, old crusties calling out at her as she squeezes between the tables.

'Where's me food?'

'I swear the sausages were bigger last time.'

'I've spilled me tea. Can I have another?'

I turn round to see a little desk that's almost hidden behind the door. And that's when I notice Daniel. He's just standing there, completely still, Monkey dangling from one hand. His eyes are closed and he's licking his lips again.

'You OK, Snotface?' I say, putting my hand on his shoulder.

He takes a deep sniff. The corners of his mouth twitch upwards.

'You like the smell, Big D?' asks Dad. He nods towards the desk. 'Shall we get some chips?'

Monkey slips out of Daniel's hand and tumbles onto the carpet.

Daniel and Monkey

I was feeling seriously Turquoise but now actually I'm NOT because the smell is so good and it is CHIPS again. And I feel all WHITE now, like waking up in my comfy bed after a SUPER-LONG LIE-IN. And I close my eyes and the smell is a cloud of LOVELINESS and there is still a tiny little bit of

Turquoise guilty feeling, but it gets smaller and smaller till it's a PINPRICK and then it disappears with a POP because how can something that smells so GOOD be BAD? And the White is bubbling up and up with Pink as well and maybe Monkey is calling my name but it's muffled and I can't feel him any more in my hand but it's OK. And when I open my eyes again the people are back.

The people!

I can see their faces and it is nice to see their faces again, like finding my favourite T-shirt at the back of the drawer.

The woman is looking at me.

I like her face. She has a big smile.

And so does the man with the beard.

And there is the girl too, and she is holding my shoulder.

And – look – even the old woman is here.

Names. I feel like I should know their names but I don't.

And the man says, WAARK WAARK WAARK get some chips.

Yes. YES. **YES**. Get some. Get some. And now the White and Pink are bursting to get out and I can't help myself any more and I yell at the top of my voice, CHHHHIIIIIIIIIIIIIPPPPPPPPPSSSSS!

Megan

The whole room stops.

Everybody stares at us.

Forks are suspended in mid-air.

Dance steps are frozen.

False teeth slip out of open mouths.

Somewhere, the waitress drops a plate and an old person swears at her.

The ancient trumpeter of the jazz band misses his note with a *pffffffffft* and falls off his chair. He lies there on the floor like a stranded tortoise, his legs waggling in the air. Glaring at us, two of the male nurses go over to help him up.

This is horrible.

Dad grins at the room. 'He likes chips,' he says nervously.

The old people go back to their food with a disapproving rumble of conversation.

'What did you do that for, Snotface?' I ask Daniel, even though actually I find it really funny.

Daniel looks spooked out, like the word was a complete shock to him. I hand Monkey back to him and he clutches it to his chest, murmuring and whimpering to it.

I try to talk to him but he won't even look at me again

now. It's so frustrating. Being with him's like watching a video on a really bad Wi-Fi signal – one minute the picture's crystal-clear HD. The next he's frozen and you don't know when he'll stop buffering.

Mum and Dad have gone over to the table behind the door. There's a lady sitting behind it with a cash box in front of her. She's about mid-fifties, big hair.

'We'd *really* like some fish and chips, please,' says Mum.

'Sorry. Over sixty-fives only,' says the lady.

Grandma sniffs. 'Well, *I* don't mind if the rest of you have to wait outside.'

Thanks a bunch.

'But you don't understand,' says Dad. 'My son needs this. We *all* need this.'

'I'm sorry,' she says. 'Those are the rules. Maximum of two carers per senior citizen. You can always come back at six.'

She holds up her hands as if to say, *what can I do?* But you can tell she loves how important this makes her feel.

'Two carers?' says Mum to Dad. 'Well, why don't you and Daniel be Grandma's carers? Megan and I can wait.'

Can we now?

My belly grumbles.

'Ooh, lovely, Karen,' says Grandma. 'I've been saying for a while I could do with a carer. Will they file my verruca down for me? My toe looks like a cauliflower. And perhaps they could bleach my knickers. They aren't quite as white as they used to be.'

I think I might hurl.

Dad ignores her. 'No. We need to be together. And we need to eat now. While he's in the right mood.'

'I'm sorry,' says the woman, her voice all syrupy. 'Two carers and that's it.'

Mum turns for the door. She's given up. I can't believe she was ever a punk. Can't believe she ever kicked a policeman up the bum or whatever it was she did. What a disappointment.

Daniel and Monkey

– What the hell did you shout that for, man? says Monkey. He is REALLY CROSS with me and I can tell this because he is bashing his hand into his fist and spit is FROTHING UP in the corner of his mouth.

– I don't know, I say, but this is not really true because I think I do know a bit. Somebody once taught me it is important to understand WHY you had a BIG MOOD and for some reason that makes me remember about the boat that bashed into me with the woman's face on it.

— Listen. Nobody screams *CHIPS!* like that for nothin', says Monkey and his voice interrupts what I am thinking about.

I say, I am sorry, Monkey. I'm not sure why I shouted *CHIPS!* like that.

And Monkey says, And what about when you dropped me, huh? What about then? I landed on my tail-hole, man. Burned like freakin' crazy!

— I'm so—

— And what did ya do? Did ya come and help me? Did ya nuts! I saw ya grinnin' at them people like a goofball.

— No, Monkey. No. It wasn't like that.

And I cuddle Monkey really TIGHT but he doesn't say anything else. And I feel so TURQUOISE I think I might blow up because I know it WAS exactly like that.

And I know exactly why I shouted *CHIPS*.

Megan

Just as Mum reaches the door, an old man swoops in front of her. He's about eighty, I reckon – slim and sprightly with thin white hair and a neatly clipped moustache. There's a row of medals pinned to his immaculate navy-blue jacket.

'Couldn't help hearing your troubles,' he says. His voice is silky. Posh.

Dad comes up alongside Mum, his head tilted to one side.

'We can't keep a family away from their supper, can we?' the old man says, aiming a playful punch at Dad's shoulder. 'I daresay I could do with a couple of extra carers . . .'

'Excuse me?' says Dad.

The old man bends double and puts on this weak, reedy voice. 'Oh I'm so elderly and frail that I need two people to hold my fork for me.' Then he straightens up, bursts into laughter and punches Dad on the arm again.

I slowly start to realise what he's on about – we can pretend to be looking after him and then we'll all be able to eat here. Not that he looks as if he needs looking after. He's got a healthy red face and twinkling little eyes.

'Very kind but there's no n—' begins Mum.

'Nonsense!' says the man, clapping his hands together. Then he calls over to the desk: 'They're with me!'

The woman behind the desk purses her lips sourly, annoyed that her authority has been yanked away from her. 'Fifty pounds for five tickets.'

'Really kind of you,' says Dad, turning to pay.

The old man snorts. 'No, no. Happy to help a family in

distress. Particularly when you've brought such a beautiful young lady with you.'

At first I think he's talking about me or Mum, and it makes me feel quite sick. But then I realise he isn't. He's looking right at Grandma.

Now I feel REALLY sick.

And you'll never guess what he does next.

He kisses her hand.

Honestly! Just like that, he swoops in, presses his lips and his clipped moustache against her gnarly old knuckles and slobbers all over them.

'Name's Frank,' says the old man, 'but you can call me the Major.'

'Oh I will,' purrs Grandma.

Gross.

Dad comes back, looking disappointed. 'They don't take cards. Have you got any cash?'

'I have,' says Grandma suddenly.

What?!!!!

Grandma has literally NEVER offered to pay for anything ever. She's the world's biggest skinflint. Dad says the last coin she used had Queen Victoria's face on it.

We all gape at her as she takes the key from round her neck, undoes the little padlock on her bumbag and rummages inside. I try to peek at what's in there but she turns her back, eventually pulling out a crumpled wad of ten-pound notes before zipping it straight back up again.

'That's it. Shut it quick before the bats escape,' says Dad, under his breath.

We find a table and sit down. The room has settled down after Daniel's outburst and, now the trumpeter's been rescued, the music's started up again. It's quite nice really. There's a white paper tablecloth on the table, and a little vase with a plastic rose in it. And I like the old people swaying about on the dance floor together. It's sweet.

I notice that Daniel has sat Monkey on the edge of the table, facing away from him. Daniel is looking in the opposite direction, bottom lip sticking out, like they've had a row.

I'm about to say something to him when the waitress comes over.

'Five fish specials, please,' Dad says, excitedly handing over the menu and our tickets. 'With three teas and a couple of cans of Fanta.'

'Not what we were expecting, but it's all right, isn't it?' asks Dad, once she's gone.

Mum glances at Grandma, who's hooting with laughter at something the Major has said. 'It's not bad, I suppose.'

'Oh my word. I'm nine months pregnant,' says Dad, resting his hands on his belly. 'And I think it's triplets.'

I know exactly how he feels. The food was *so* good and there was *so* much of it. My tummy is straining against my jeans and there's grease all round my mouth. A couple of tiny, crispy scraps are all that's left on my plate. I'd eat them but I reckon I might actually explode and shower the roomful of old people with the contents of my stomach.

'Best so far,' sighs Dad. 'Ten out of ten.'

'Mnyammm,' I say in agreement.

We've eaten fish and chips a million times, but this was a whole different level to anything we've ever had before. The third best chippy in the country and it was *incredible*: the chunkiest fish, the lightest batter, the featheriest chips, the meatiest gravy.

'Admit it,' Dad says to Mum. 'Just this once I got it right.'

'Just this once,' she agrees, hands behind her head. 'Ten from me too.'

Dad holds his hand out to her. Mum smiles and reaches over to squeeze it.

Wow! The grub was so good it's even perked *her* up. But it wasn't the best thing about the meal.

The best thing was Daniel.

When the food arrived, Monkey was still facing away from him. Daniel slowly and carefully sneaked a chip into his mouth before quickly chewing and swallowing.

I looked at him as if to say, *What are you doing, you weirdo?*

He made a shush sign again. But this time, there was real pleading in his eyes. Almost like he was begging me.

I was desperate to talk to him, but I didn't want to break the spell. Instead I watched, amazed and slightly amused, as he carried on furtively gobbling chips.

As soon as he'd finished, he grabbed my plate, stacked it on top of his and shoved it back into my place. Then he wiped his hands on the seat, gulped down some Fanta and turned Monkey back round. Straight away he started muttering to it again, and he's still at it now.

'Ten from me too,' Grandma says, letting out a little burp.

'And *you* get a ten from me!' the Major says, twirling his moustache at her.

For some reason, watching these two old codgers flirting doesn't make me feel quite so ill now. Maybe it's the food, or how happy I am about Daniel.

I reckon Daniel would give the chips a nine. He seems to have enjoyed them, but he's been a bit stressed out about the whole thing.

Forty-nine out of fifty. We have a new leader!

I watch the old people limp round the dance floor as I wipe up a smear of tomato sauce from my plate with one of my crispy scraps. Then I pop the scrap into my mouth. Who cares if I explode?

Daniel and Monkey

Monkey was cross at me. While his back was turned I ate a delicious plate of fish and chips NINJA-STYLE so he didn't know about it, and he didn't move EVEN ONE TINY TOENAIL.

And the funny thing was that while I was eating my chips I could see the faces – Old Lady, Girl, Woman, Man with Beard – and I had the super-warm WHITE feeling again, like when you sit in front of the fire on a snowy day.

And my favourite one is the girl, I think. And I gave her a HUSH sign so she didn't tell Monkey about the chips and she smiled and I think I almost remembered something but then it went again and I carried on GOBBLING my chips.

Then the millisecond after I swallowed the last one, Monkey turned round and said, C'mon, man. What we fighting for? Let's be buddies again.

And I gave him a HIGH FIVE.

And he said, Why don't we pretend we're in Egypt and we're surrounded by crusty old mummies?

And I wanted things to be like NORMAL, even though I'd just eaten the chips and I didn't want him to know, so I said, yes, and crusty old daddies too.

And Monkey LAUGHED and said, D-Bop-a-Loo-Bop, you're one funny dude!

Then I looked over to the girl but I couldn't see her face any more and that made me feel sad.

Megan

The Major claps Dad on the shoulder. 'So what brings you to these parts?'

'Well. Actually, we're touring the best chip shops in Britain,' says Dad.

'Ha ha! Sounds like a lark!' says the Major. 'And why not, eh? Seize the day. That's what I say. You can't afford to hang around when you're my age. You might be bones in a box tomorrow.'

What a jolly thought.

'I couldn't agree more,' says Grandma. 'I'm here even though I'm a very sick woman – arthritis of the appendix and a flaky bladder, among many other ailments. Not that I like to make a fuss, of course.'

I let this go.

The Major nods wisely. 'And are these your grand-children? Hello there, young fellow. How are you?'

Daniel says nothing. He's still in deep conversation with Monkey, who's now sitting on his lap.

'He had a terrible accident,' says Grandma. She tries to mouth it but it comes out really loud. 'Only speaks to his cuddly toy these days.'

Daniel doesn't react. He's gone right back within himself since finishing his food. I guess we'll have to get used to this. Small steps though, right?

'Goodness,' says the Major. 'Well, it is a fine toy.'

'I bought it for him in New York,' says Grandma. 'I was on holiday with my husband, just before he died. Young Daniel was born a month early while we were out there.'

I stop and look at her.

I'd no idea that it was *her* who bought Monkey. No idea that she'd ever travelled anywhere. She never talks about my grandad. I hardly remember him – he died just after Daniel was born.

'Yes,' she says. Her voice is so much softer than normal. 'You do get lonely from time to time.'

Mum looks sadly at Grandma.

The Major pats her hand, and immediately I understand that he knows exactly what she means. Knows what it's like to be alone. Has he lost *his* wife too? I feel sad for him.

Then he suddenly perks up. 'Would you do me the honour of a waltz?' he says. 'I've just had a new hip and I need a beautiful young lady to try it out on.'

Wow! *Nice chat-up line, Mr Smooth!* That's got to be up there w th: 'Give me a kiss before I pop my clogs.'

'Well!' splutters Grandma. 'I've not been asked to dance in fifty years.'

'About time you said yes then,' says the Major. 'Seize the day.'

And before I know it, the old geezer's pulled her out of her seat and up onto the dance floor. And now she's shuffling about with him, one hand clasped in his, the other on his back, her bumbag keeping their waists apart.

'Is this happening?' I say to Dad.

'I honestly don't know,' he replies. 'Maybe I've eaten so much I'm hallucinating.'

'What's she doing?' says Mum.

'I think . . . Grandma's . . . *pulled,*' I say.

Goggle-eyed, we watch her for a few minutes. As she dances a sparkly joy just seems to shine from her eyes. I find myself smiling. And, when I look at Mum and Dad, they're smiling too, and holding hands.

'Ahh, Mum,' says my mum, as Grandma slowly whirls past. She looks as if she might cry.

Dad stands up and pushes his chair back. He pulls the plastic rose out of the little vase, clamps it between his teeth, stamps his foot and pretends to play the castanets. 'Beautiful-a laydee. You wish for to make-a the dance?' he says in this rubbish Spanish accent.

Before Mum can answer, he's swept her out of her chair and he's spinning her across the floor. Her head tilts back as she whoops with laughter. 'Go, Mum! Go, Dad!' I holler over to them.

I know I should be embarrassed, and normally I'd be hiding under the table. But it's the loveliest feeling ever watching them happy together after everything that's happened, and I don't care that the rest of the miserable old people are all giving them evils and hobbling back to their tables, moaning. It's beautiful, absolutely beautiful and . . . *oh why not?*

I haul Daniel out of his chair and drag him onto the dance floor. 'Come on, Snotface. Let's have a dance!'

To my total surprise, he follows me, tripping over his own feet.

Daniel

I was talking to Monkey and then a hand GRABBED me and PULLED me out of my seat and I was like, WOAH! WHAT ARE YOU DOING? But then I saw it was the girl – the one with the nice HEAD. Her face had come back and it made me feel pink happy to see her.

Now she's holding my hands and MOVING them forward and back, forward and back. And she has a funny, silly smile on her face and there is MUSIC and I smile back at her and move my feet and my head and I think we are DANCING.

Megan

I can't believe it. I'm dancing with Daniel.

And he's dancing back.

It's amazing! I'm sticking my tongue out at him and doing silly moves – all twiddly fingers and bouncy knees. And he's enjoying it too – trying to copy but lagging behind the music, his hands and feet not quite keeping up.

'That's it, Daniel!' I say, a big grin almost splitting my face in two.

And then just like that he stops.

Freezes.

His eyes widen.

'Are you OK?' I say. Is he scared? Worried? He doesn't have Monkey with him. I look around for it, but he's still staring at me. A look of concentration comes across his face.

And I freeze too.

Because I've seen that look before, a million times, back before the accident. It's the look he gives when Dad asks him to remember everything we've done on a day out, or when I'm helping him with his maths homework, or when he's deciding which chip shop we should try next.

For a moment it's like a haunting reminder of who he was. Who he used to be. The dance floor with the old people and Mum and Dad and Grandma and the Major fade away. The music goes silent in my head. It's just me and him. Me and my brother. My legs suddenly feel very weak.

'Go on, Daniel,' I say, barely daring to breathe. 'What is it?'

His pupils get bigger in those beautiful, brown eyes of his. And he slowly purses his lips together.

Daniel

We were dancing, me and the girl. And then she said Daniel which is ME. And she pulled a funny face.

And suddenly all these PICTURES came into my brain.

In a wood somewhere – like a school or something – and I'm crying and sad and DARK RED AND BLACK ANGRY with no shoes and pushing a stick in my eye and the girl is holding me tight and telling me everything's all right, and another picture which is a TIFFCAT with the woman from the front of the boat and another picture of FISH AND CHIPS in a steamy, foggy kitchen and LAUGHING, LAUGHING with Girl and Man and Woman and Old Woman too.

And then I remember it. I remember her name.

Megan

'Mmmmegan,' he whispers.

I can't reply.

He said my name.

My knees give way and I'm down on the floor and I'm hugging him round his legs and I'm crying, absolutely bawling.

'Yes!' I say, the snot and tears catching in my throat. 'Yes, Daniel! It's me, Megan!'

And I feel Mum and Dad behind me and the music has stopped and they're asking me what's wrong and I can't say it. Can't put it into words.

'Megan,' he says again.

Mum's hand is over her mouth and Dad's laughing and pumping his fists. 'Get in there, Big D!'

'M-um-my,' says Daniel, rolling the word around his mouth. 'D-ad-dy.'

And Mum and Dad grab him in a hug and we're all there, together, finally. Holding each other, relief and happiness and tears and love pouring between us like this enormous river bursting its banks.

Daniel

The girl called Megan is on her knees and the man and the woman called Daddy and Mummy are laughing and smiling and hugging me and it is nice and SUPER-WHITE.

But then another picture SUDDENLY comes into my head.

And the picture is:

MUMMY AND DADDY AND MEGAN AND ME AND THE OLD WOMAN WHOSE NAME IS ACTUALLY GRANDMA.

FISH AND CHIPS.

BLUE MOOD.

BRIGHT LIGHTS.

LOUD *SCREECH*.

LOUD *THUNK*

AND HURTY PAIN

I don't know why, but it makes me feel WOBBLY and I need Monkey so I say, Monkey? Monkey?

And I realise he is not in my hand.

Megan

Out of nowhere, Daniel screams.

It's sudden and awful, full of anguish and pain. Instinctively we all relax our grip on him and he wriggles out from the group hug and stares savagely at us. His eyes are wild, his hands balled into tight fists.

He barges past us over to the table then he screams again and starts smacking himself hard in the eyes and face, each punch landing with a sickening crack of bone and flesh.

What on earth is wrong with him?

Then I realise.

Our table has been cleared.

And Monkey's gone.

We're back in the car.

It didn't take *long* to find Monkey after we'd realised he was lost – maybe thirty seconds – but that thirty seconds felt like an eternity.

Daniel was having the worst meltdown I think I've ever seen – raining punches into his own face, clawing at his eyes, pulling clumps of hair out, biting his fingers, kicking the tables.

I had to sprint over and pin his arm down to stop him from stabbing a fork into his face.

It reminded me of being six again – holding on to him in the little wooded area at school during his first week while he shoved sticks in his eyes. Back before MrsMaryWoodcock came along.

But this time he didn't want my comfort. He flung an

elbow at me. There was an explosion of pain under my eye and I fell back. He glared at me – pure hatred burning out of him, his jaw clenched and his chest heaving. His cheeks were red and swollen from where he'd smacked them.

In that moment, all my hope, all my happiness, evaporated.

'Here you go, little fellow,' said the Major, waving the cuddly toy towards Daniel. 'Found it in the bin bag. No harm done. Silly beggars hadn't been looking at what they were throwing away.'

Daniel snatched it off him, then crawled to the corner of the room and cuddled it tightly under his duffel coat.

'Calm down. It's just a toy,' said the Major, surprised.

Just a toy.

Daniel and Monkey

– Look. You understand why I hit ya, doncha? says Monkey.

– Because you were mad? I say.

– Damn right I was mad. But I did it cos I love ya, buddy.

It's a bit of time since I lost Monkey and then found him again. We stayed in that place for a while but now we are back in the car again. My face is SORE and SWOLLEN and my knuckles are RED and BLEEDING. One of my eyes doesn't OPEN very much.

Monkey sighs at me all HUFFY and he says, Look, man, I'm sorry. But sometimes a monkey's gotta crack some skulls, know what I'm sayin'?

And even though I didn't like it when he was beating me up, I look at the floor of the car and I say, I understand, Monkey. I deserved it.

— Someone needed to knock some sense into ya, kid. Ya left me for dead and ya went dancin' with that dumb broad.

I try to imagine the face of the girl whose name is Megan, but it disappears like SAND through my FINGERS.

This makes me Grey sad but I don't tell Monkey.

He sighs again. Look, D-Funk. I don't blame ya for it, ya know that? They hypnotised ya. Brainwashed ya with the French fries and the dancin' and all that garbage. I warned ya about 'em right from the start. But ya didn't listen. We almost lost each other back there, buddy. I had to hit ya to make ya realise.

— I'm sorry, Monkey, I say, and I feel Turquoise and Grey at the same time.

– I need ya, kid. I told ya a billion times – I can't cope on my own since my accident.

When he says about his accident, I get that PICTURE in my head again, of the LIGHTS and the SCREECH.

I shiver, and Monkey says, C'mon. Gimme a hug.

I cuddle him so tight I think he might burst, because I am trying to get rid of the HORRIBLE PICTURE in my head.

He smells strong of fish and chips but I don't like the smell any more. It's horrible. It's disgusting. It's like DOG POO wrapped in BURNT HAIR and dipped in SICK.

I AM NEVER GOING NEAR THE GIRL CALLED MEGAN AND THE MAN AND WOMAN CALLED MUMMY AND DADDY EVER AGAIN. Their faces have gone away now, and now it's just Monkey and me again, ALONE like it should be.

Megan

It took over an hour for him to calm down. Everyone else had long since left the restaurant by then. The Major stayed on with Grandma, whispering and laughing together. The rest of us sat awkwardly at the next table as the room was cleared and reset, and the evening diners started to dribble in.

Eventually Daniel had calmed down enough for us to be able to lead him out quietly. You might think we'd be glad about this. But after he'd said our names just an hour before, it was seriously depressing. He was back to his old zombie state – not recognising us, not even acknowledging our existence, his eyes glassy and his face blank.

We trudged back to the car and we've been driving ever since, whizzing through the dark along country lanes between high hedges that seem to be swallowing us up.

The Major didn't want to leave Grandma, so she offered him a lift and he told his bus driver to go back to the old people's home without him. The bus driver looked worried but the Major said he'd survived parachute drops under enemy machine gun fire and he could manage to find his way home with a beautiful woman. He's in the passenger seat on account of his new hip. I'm in the middle row, with Mum and Grandma either side of me. We folded out the boot seats and Daniel's back there, a million miles away in his own universe.

'Are you sure this is right?' says Dad. The words make me jump. Apart from Daniel grunting at Monkey, nobody's said a single word since we set off.

The Major doesn't answer him. He fell asleep soon after

we left the restaurant and he's still snoring.

'Don't disturb him,' says Grandma. 'He's resting. Use your who-jammy-do-dah instead.'

'No signal out here,' says Mum.

'Can I not just wake him up?' asks Dad. 'Coo-ee!'

'What? Who?' says the Major with a start. 'Did I drift off for a moment?'

'Course not,' says Grandma, which technically isn't a lie. He drifted off for flipping ages.

'Are we going the right way?' asks Dad again.

'Yes. Follow the road. Can't miss it,' says the Major. Then he sniffs and looks out of the window. 'Er . . . where are we exactly?'

Dad swears under his breath. 'We're on the valley road. The one you sent me down out of the village.'

'That's right. Twenty-five miles along here.'

'Twenty-five miles?!' cries Dad, slapping the steering wheel. 'Jeez. Thanks for letting us know beforehand.'

'Everything's twenty-five miles away in the countryside,' says Grandma, but I don't think this can be true.

'I'll walk if it's too much trouble,' says the Major.

Dad slows down and starts indicating off the road. Mum tuts, so he speeds up again, muttering under his breath.

'You stay right where you are, Major,' says Grandma. 'We're thoroughly enjoying your company.'

Bit of an exaggeration.

The Major yawns and rubs the back of his neck. 'I do apologise. I've come over awfully tired.'

'Must be all that dancing,' coos Grandma. 'You're quite a mover. I'd have danced with you all night, if it wasn't for my ulcerated kneecaps of course.'

I say nothing.

The Major turns round. 'You were a marvellous partner. And we'll certainly dance together again. Seize the day. Make the most of every breath, I say.'

And, with that, he falls fast asleep again.

'Too true,' says Grandma, her voice a big smile in the dark. 'Too true.'

At least somebody's happy, I think, rubbing my face, which is still tender from where Daniel whacked me.

Daniel and Monkey

Monkey and me are STILL cuddling, and I want this to last FOREVER.

— You sure there's nothin' else worryin' ya, Big D? says Monkey.

And I cough and then say, ACTUALLY, yes, there is.

Because I've decided that I am NEVER going to

lie to Monkey ever again. I have been BAD but now
I will be GOOD.

— You can tell me, man.

I gulp and I say, well, the thing is that I keep
getting this PICTURE in my HEAD.

Monkey pulls away from me and looks at me over
his sunglasses. What kinda picture? he asks.

— It's a picture which is VERY REALISTIC because
it has sounds and feelings too: BRIGHT LIGHTS and
a SCREECH and BAD PAIN. I got it earlier, and again
just now when you said about your accident. I
think I was thinking about a car.

And Monkey goes stiff and then he says, I don't
think you should be thinkin' about that sorta
stuff, D-Funk. Ain't good for ya.

— It feels like maybe I was in an accident TOO,
Monkey. Was I?

Monkey stares at me for a moment. Then he
blows out his lips and he says, That ain't possible,
man. You ain't got no injuries. Just look at my
butt. It was me who got hit by the car, right? I
don't even know where my tail is no more.

He bends over to show me. The stuffing is
hanging out of his bum where his tail should be so I
push it back in again.

— You're RIGHT, Monkey, I know you are.

– You wanna know what it is, man? You're such a great guy and we're such great buddies that ya remember what happened to me as if it happened to YOU. It's like we're one and the same. Brothers from another mother, right?

– Right.

– We're so tight that it's like you were there. But you weren't. It was me. I got hit by the car. Not you. Just remember that, OK?

This sort of makes me feel better, but also makes me think about something else.

– But how can I be sure if I can't REMEMBER much about ANYTHING? I say.

– Why doncha let me do the rememberin' from now on, huh?

I don't answer.

And Monkey says, Look. Just cos them putzes have been stuffin' ya full of French fries and bad ideas, you're startin' to doubt your own brain. I mean, you almost ditched your best pal back there.

My tummy clenches with TURQUOISE again. Sorry, I say.

– Quit sayin' sorry. Just stick with me. I'll look after ya. Hey – ever been swimmin' under a waterfall? Nobody can get near ya there. C'mon.

And we're suddenly in a CAVE with a ROARING

CURTAIN of water pouring down in front of us, which cuts us off and PROTECTS us from the rest of the world.

— We're safe here. Why doncha take a nap? I'll keep lookout, says Monkey.

Megan

After another twenty minutes we see a large sign at the side of the road: 'The Last Post – Rest Home for Ex-Servicemen'.

Dad swings off the road and rolls up onto a gravel driveway in front of a big, white-painted old house. 'All right, old fella. Wake up. We're here,' he says briskly.

The Major doesn't move.

'Major,' says Grandma. 'I say, Major – you're home.'

'Come on,' says Dad. 'I'm not carrying you up to bed.'

The Major doesn't move.

'Major?' says Grandma, rubbing his arm. Then again, more urgently. 'Major?'

The Major slumps forward in his seat.

Grandma breathes in sharply.

'How's Daniel?' Mum asks.

'He's still asleep across the back seat, cuddling Monkey,' replies Dad. He walks across the waiting room and slumps down onto one of the low armchairs. 'I locked the car door so nobody can steal him.'

Mum doesn't laugh. 'Grandma wanted to sit with the Major. You know, before they . . . take him away.'

Dad nods, then turns to me. 'How are you doing, Meg?'

I shrug. I'm OK, I guess. Well, apart from the obvious.

After a while Grandma shuffles into the room, along with a male nurse.

'Stay for as long as you like,' says the nurse kindly. 'Help yourself to tea and toast. You've had a nasty shock. And you never get used to it, I'm afraid.'

'Thanks,' says Grandma, and she sits on the chair next to Mum, her hands fumbling with a shredded tissue.

The nurse leaves us and closes the door behind him.

Nobody says anything for a while. Outside the room, a policewoman goes past the window, talking to a man with a stethoscope round his neck. They both wave briefly to Grandma, and then they're gone.

Grandma bites her lip. 'We'll probably need to speak to the police again at some point, but the doctor said it'll just be a formality. Wasn't suspicious, see. Apparently the Major had a bad heart. Could've happened any time. They'd warned him about fatty foods and dancing, but he didn't listen. Said he wanted to have fun while he still could.'

We all nod, looking at the floor. I feel bad for the Major. It must be terrible, knowing you could die at any moment. No wonder he kept going on about making the most of his life. *Seize the day*, right? It might be your last one.

'I'd like to go to the funeral, if that's OK. He didn't have a family,' says Grandma eventually. 'Sad to think of someone not having a family, isn't it?'

Mum clasps Grandma's hand.

There's another long silence, then Grandma pats her bumbag. 'You know why I carry this everywhere with me?'

'You couldn't find a suitcase big enough?' asks Dad, trying to break the mood.

'No, cheeky,' says Grandma. 'It's for keeping things close to me.'

She opens it up and sifts through the usual rubbish – a pair of glasses, a packet of pear drops, an old disposable camera, a bag of coins. But then a flash of pink-and-yellow stripes catches my eye. It looks familiar, but before I can see it properly she zips the bumbag up again.

'Here you go,' she says, passing round a little plastic wallet stuffed full of photos.

They're amazing – pictures from ages ago when everyone

was younger: Mum and Dad on their wedding day – Dad with a scruffy beard and tight brown suit, Mum in a black dress and green boots with purple hair and spiky earrings sticking out everywhere. Dad's holding a tray of chips and Mum's pouting at the camera, pinching one off him.

'What's with the chips?' I ask.

'You know that chip van where they met each other?' says Grandma. 'They had it come and do the food for the wedding.'

Mum looks like she's disappointed with herself for that, but I think chips on your wedding day sounds brilliant.

Grandma turns past a few more. 'Here's the one I was looking for.'

It's a picture of her on a boat in front of the Statue of Liberty. She looks plumper and less wrinkly, like a slightly inflated version of herself today, and her hair's blacker. Next to her is a beaming old man. My grandad.

Mum lets out a tiny choked sob and covers her mouth with her hand.

'This is when we went to New York,' said Grandma. 'Remember, Jim – you phoned the hotel to tell us Daniel had been born. We went straight out when we got the message and bought the toy monkey for him that day.'

She and Mum sigh together.

'He died about two weeks after this photo,' continues Grandma. 'Just after we got back and met Daniel for the first time. Tonight – meeting the Major, dancing, what *happened* . . . It's just brought back memories, that's all.'

We s t there for ages, thinking and not talking.

Then, after a long time, Mum stands up. 'Come on then. Shall we go home?'

We all turn to look at her.

'Home?' I ask.

'We can't,' says Dad, his voice almost a whine. 'We've still got two chip shops to go to.'

'You're not serious?' says Mum. 'After everything that's happened today?'

'But . . .'

Mum's lips go pale. 'Jim. It's almost 2 a.m. Mum's friend's just died. Daniel's sleeping off the biggest emotional crisis of his life. We're going home. Now. And tomorrow, we're calling that clinic and Daniel is going there as soon as possible.'

'You said we'd keep going till there's no more hope.'

'There *is* no more hope!' snaps Mum, pinching her nose. 'Daniel's mashed his face up. Mum's upset. We're all shattered. I'm getting in the car and I'm driving to our house. You can join me or you can walk.'

She spins on her heel and sweeps towards the door.

Dad gulps a few times, flapping his arms, before he follows her. Grandma heaves herself out of the chair.

Then something bursts up out of me.

'STOP!' I shout. 'You can't just give up. We've not finished yet.'

Mum takes a deep breath and faces me wearily. 'Megan. I'm tired. Please.'

'No,' I say. 'If we go home now, then we've not fixed anything.'

'The clinic might fix Dan—'

'But it won't fix *us*. Look at us. We *need* to go to the last two chip shops.'

Mum puts her hands on her hips. 'What? Why?'

'Well . . . I mean . . .' I splutter.

Mum purses her lips at me. It's funny because she's got the exact same expression on her face as in her wedding photo – defiant, almost daring someone to argue with her.

And then something hits me.

The wedding photo.

Of course.

Oh my word – how did it take me this long to figure it out?! What an idiot! Now it all makes sense. The trip. The list Dad stuck into Daniel's notebook. Everything.

'Go on. Why?' repeats Mum.

'Because . . .' I begin. I look at Dad, and something in his eyes stops me from explaining the whole thing right there and then. 'Because . . . it's IMPORTANT. And I'm *not* going home.'

'Megan. Get in the car now.'

'No.'

'Excuse me?'

Now that I understand everything, I feel this sudden rush of confidence. I've found my voice. 'I'm fed up of being ignored. I'm fed up of nobody paying any attention to me. What are you going to do? Leave me here in the middle of nowhere at this time of night? I'm not going back home till I've been to those last two chip shops.'

'Just like her mother,' Dad whispers, sounding amazed.

'We agreed,' says Mum, trying not to yell at me. 'We go home when there's no more hope.'

'Hope?' I say. 'Daniel looked in my eyes. He said my name. And he said yours, remember.'

'Yeah. Just before he lost it and nearly broke his own jaw.'

'Well, guess what? That's Daniel, isn't it? That's what he used to do before the accident. He flipped out sometimes. His moods went up and down. Doesn't that tell you he's getting a little bit better?'

'Megan. Listen to me –'

'No. You listen to me for once. If we want Daniel back, we're going to have to get used to that sort of stuff. He's not perfect. He never has been.'

'Stop it. This isn't the time or the place –'

But I won't stop it. Not till I've finished. 'Families aren't perfect either. And for two minutes back there, we were a family again. We're not giving up just like that.'

Mum grits her teeth. 'Get. In. The. Car.'

Grandma hobbles up and puts her arm round me. At first I think she's going to lead me outside, but then she sets her jaw and says, 'No! Megan's right. And so was the Major.'

Mum's neck is going blotchy. 'Mum,' she splutters. 'This is ridiculous.'

Grandma squeezes my shoulder, and I realise that maybe she understands everything as well. 'We're seizing the day, dammit. And we're going for some chips. Fire up the engine, Jim.'

'Aye aye, captain,' grins Dad, and he tosses his keys in the air and catches them, shrugging at Mum as he ducks out of the room.

Nine o'clock in the morning. Still a hundred and fifty miles from London.

We drove for a while then stopped at another cheap hotel near a town on the way. Dad had to carry Daniel in and lay him on the bed. He woke up this morning with a real panic – terrified by the unfamiliar room - before burying his head in Monkey and closing his eyes till we reached the car.

Now we're moving again.

Mum's dozing in the front. I don't think she slept.

Grandma and I are looking out of our windows. Even though there's a space next to me, Daniel's stayed in the back, grumbling to Monkey and sucking its hand. Dad's cheerfully whistling along to Radio 2.

I turn around to Daniel. 'Hey, Snotface,' I say. There's no response from his eyes but I don't give up. 'We're going to London now. You know, Buckingham Palace. Soldiers with funny hats. Red buses. And we're going for fish and chips. Twice!' Am I imagining it or did the tiniest tip of his tongue just emerge and lick his lips? I carry on. 'The best two places in the country. One's meant to be super-cool. And the other is . . . well. It's a surprise. You'll love it.'

He says nothing.

'Breakfast?' says Dad from the front, his voice full of happiness as he indicates into a supermarket car park.

Daniel and Monkey

— Did I do OK, Monkey? I ask, because I was TRYING MY BESTEST to not listen to the girl called MEGAN. I couldn't see her face still, but her voice wasn't just WAARK WAARK WAARK — it was actually words like LONDON and CHIPS, and when she said CHIPS I might have accidentally LICKED MY

LIPS although I didn't want to, which is called an INVOLUNTARY REACTION, like when you sneeze or yawn. I didn't lick my lips for long though because then she said SURPRISE and I don't like surprises, like when a spider crawls at you or when you see LIGHTS and hear SCREECHING BRAKES.

I shiver and try to stop thinking about that PICTURE IN MY HEAD.

– Kid, you were perfect, says Monkey, which he says like POIFECT, and he gives me a high five.

I feel white that Monkey likes me again and it takes my mind off the picture.

– Happy, buddy? he says.

– YES! I say, loud but hopefully NOT so quickly that he knows I was thinking of CHIPS and SURPRISES and PICTURES in my head.

– Me too. Hey. Pull my finger . . .

I pull on Monkey's hand and he lets out the biggest, longest, squealiest trump in the history of the world ever.

I laugh a lot but then Monkey says, Now THAT'S what I call an involuntary reaction.

I stop laughing STRAIGHT AWAY. Did Monkey know that this is exactly what I was thinking a moment ago, or is it just a coincidence? I don't like the idea of Monkey being able to read my mind.

He carries on laughing though and he says, Sometimes it helps to have a big hole in your butt, know what I'm sayin'? Man. I nearly lost my stuffin'.

And I swallow hard and smile a BIT WEAKLY and say, That was a beauty.

Then he gets SERIOUS and he says, Look, D-Man, we have good times, right?

— Yes, I say, happy to not think about if he can SEE INSIDE MY HEAD or not.

— And we love each other, right?

— Yes!

— We're gonna have a real time in London, man. A real time. All you gotta do is keep bein' my buddy. Promise?

— Promise.

— Well, come on then. Whatcha waitin' for? Let's find a secret hideout.

And he crawls under my duffel coat.

For a moment I stop and think about what the girl called Megan said about LONDON and CHIPS and I lick my lips again, but then I start to get BRIGHT RED angry at myself because I shouldn't be thinking about those things, especially if Monkey can read my mind. Then I take a big gulp of air and follow Monkey under my coat.

Your Guide to the Best
Fish and Chip Shops in the UK

2) FNC, Camden Town, London

This uber-cool hipster venue boldly claims to have reinvented fish and chips for the twenty-first century. In the words of Head Chef, Xavier Prince: 'We ripped up the rule book to create a dining experience like no other.'

We won't spoil the surprise, but expect the unexpected and prepare to have your minds – and taste buds – blown.

Megan

It's been a long day. Mum and Daniel both refused to get out of the car for breakfast. Daniel was buried under his duffel coat and Mum had woken up and decided she wasn't talking to anyone. She reckons we bullied her into coming.

After we'd eaten, Grandma wanted to light a candle for the Major. We drove for ages before we found a church. Daniel and Mum stayed in the car again. Unfortunately they didn't have any candles in the church, so Grandma pulled a large birthday candle out of her bumbag. This kind of thing no longer surprises me. She melted the end with a cigarette lighter (also from her bumbag, even though she's never smoked) and stuck it to a bench.

'You can't use that,' I said.

'And whyever not?'

'Er. Because it says *Birthday Girl* on it in massive pink letters, perhaps?'

'Still a candle,' insisted Grandma, lighting it. To make things worse, it turned out that it was of those spitting, sparkling ones. It didn't exactly produce a solemn moment.

'God? I say, God, are you there?' she announced, her voice echoing round the cold empty room along with the hissing and crackling of the candle. She turned to me and

Dad. 'I don't know what to say next.'

I shrugged.

'Don't ask me,' said Dad. 'I'm rubbish at that sort of thing.'

Grandma scowled and puffed up her chest. 'Lord, extinguisheth not this candle like you extinguishethed the life of the Major.'

Extinguishethed?

The candle continued to spit.

'You're making it sound like God murdered him,' whispered Dad.

'Shut it, you!' snapped Grandma. 'Sorry, God. My son-in-law is an idiot. May this candle burneth eternally.'

'Or until it melts anyway,' said Dad.

Grandma slapped him. 'Amen. Let us go in peace.'

Then she bustled out again with her stick. I blew the candle out to stop it from burning the church down. Then I said inside my head, 'Even though I might not always believe in you, please help Daniel get better and bring our family back together too. Amen.'

I followed them back outside.

Daniel and Monkey

CLACKETY-CLACK. CLACKETY-CLACK. The next station is Hendon Central. CLACKETY-CLACK.

Monkey says, We're in London, baby! Great city. Reminds me of home.

He opens his jacket and pats his I HEART NEW YORK T-shirt. We're on a train, which is LOUD and SMELLY and BUSY with PEOPLE.

I try to look FEARLESS, but REALLY I feel Bright Orange TERRIFIED. The train is noisy and full of PEOPLE and probably GERMS. There is a COLOURFUL MAP on the wall though and I look at that to CALM ME DOWN a bit.

— Scared, huh? Kiss my hand, man, says Monkey.

I do as I'm told, which makes me feel a LOT BETTER. Then I have a THINK in my BRAIN. And then I remember before when he said about the INVOLUNTARY REACTION and I decide to FIND SOMETHING OUT. So I say, Monkey, how did you know I'm scared? Can you . . . READ MY MIND?

Monkey lowers his sunglasses and looks at me. Why? Anythin' up in that big melon of yours that ya don't want me to know about?

I SPLUTTER because I've been thinking LOTS of things that I don't want him to know about.

— Ah! I'm kiddin' ya, man. Sure we got a connection. But I ain't gonna do nothin' you don't want me to, right?

— Right, I say, and I smile a bit.

Then he rubs his hands together and he says, A monkey could easily get himself lost in a big city like this.

Before I can ask him what he means, the train goes into a TUNNEL, which makes it all CLATTERY and LOUD and DARK and my ears pop.

Then the girl called Megan rubs my hand and says, Don't worry, Snotface. We're going for chips.

And I get that pain in my tummy again, SUPER-HUNGRY, and I remember all the chips I've eaten this week, and then I try NOT to remember them because I'm worried Monkey will know, but the hunger is BURNING and it's like a new colour, like a flashing purple with yellow stars or something. And the more I think about it, the more I remember the dancing and the food and the white I got from seeing the girl called Megan, and I love Monkey, but if he's promised that he won't do anything I don't want him to do then maybe . . .

— Monkey. Do you want to play a game?

Megan

So Daniel's acting odd. Well, even more odd than usual.

He's got Monkey facing away from him again – just like he did last night at the restaurant – and now he's frowning really hard at the back of its head and holding up two fingers. Then he turns Monkey around and mutters into its ear. A few seconds later he does the exact same thing again but with three fingers this time.

I'm worried that people will stare at him, but Dad says nobody looks at anyone else on the tube.

'You OK, Snotface?' I ask.

Daniel seems shocked and guilty, like that time last year I caught him stealing Kit Kats from Mum's secret stash. He covers Monkey's eyes and ears with his hand, and he looks at me sideways, from under his eyelashes, as though he's trying not to. His face turns bright red, like he's seriously straining, and he actually begins to shake. Then, so quiet I can barely hear him, he whispers, 'When chips?'

And just then the train bursts out of the tunnel and back into sunshine.

Daniel and Monkey

I tried a test with Monkey.

I think he can read my mind, which is very CREEPY because I am worried he will HATE me if I think BAD THINGS. But then I did a test which was to hold up fingers behind his back and concentrate VERY HARD on stopping him from reading my thoughts.

And it worked.

Monkey giggled and got it wrong every time, which shows I can block his PSYCHIC POWERS if I want to.

So I did a naughty thing. I covered his eyes and ears, and I blocked his PSYCHIC POWERS again, and then I looked at the girl called Megan, and I realised I could see her face except today it was different because she had a BLACK EYE, which made me feel TURQUOISE GUILTY for some reason. And I asked her when can we have chips? and she said soon and then she tried to hug me again but I said NO and now I am going to take my hands off Monkey's eyes and ears. I will have to think about how I can eat the chips without him knowing about it. And I can't think about them once my hand is off his eyes because he will know WHAT I AM THINKING.

Megan

'Hey,' I say, turning from Daniel to everyone else. 'Did you hear that?'

'Keep going!' says Dad. 'He seems to really want to talk to you!'

'Seize the day!' Grandma grins.

Mum doesn't respond though. She's looking out of the window, lost in her own thoughts as we rattle in towards the city.

Dad seems to notice this too. 'Nice to be back in London, Karen?'

'Hmm,' says Mum.

'Shall we go straight to this FNC place for some food?'

'Whatever.'

The train goes underground again.

Daniel and Monkey

— Hey, D-Namite. See if that nasty broad'll give ya her phone, says Monkey.

— Why? I say.

I am surprised. Monkey does not normally want me to talk to the girl called Megan. We got off the train and we went up a LONG ESCALATOR and then we had to put a ticket in these special gates that let us through — FA-JUNK — and now we are in a big space with lots of people RUSHING ABOUT. I feel Orange scared AND Purple nervous but Monkey seems very HAPPY.

— The phone's got a map in case we decide to get lost, says Monkey.

And so I say, Why would we DECIDE to do that?

Monkey laughs. Slip of the tongue, man. I didn't mean to say that. Maybe when I got hit by that car a bit of my brain fell out of my booty.

I smile but I have SOME THINGS I am worried about.

— Hey, Monkey. Would you like to ride in my pocket? I say.

— Sure.

I put him in there so I can think about the
THINGS without Monkey knowing about them. I
don't like doing this, but my head is OVERCROWDED
and CLATTERY like that train we were just on so I
NEED some space to THINK.

Here are the THINGS that are making me Purple
nervous right now:

- That is twice that Monkey has said he wants
  to get lost. I don't like the idea of being LOST
  in this BUSY CITY, even with Monkey.
- I am so HUNGRY I could eat a SKUNK'S
  UNDERPANTS and I am SUPER-BLUE excited
  about CHIPS, but I am worried I will have to LIE
  to him so I can eat them without him knowing.

I look at the girl called Megan and I can see
her face, which is nice, and I SUDDENLY REALISE
something: I can only see her face clearly when I
am not talking to Monkey.

Thinking about Monkey makes me Turquoise
guilty so I take him back out of my pocket.

— Phone, please, I say to the girl called Megan,
but I don't look at her face.

Megan

It never stops being surprising and amazing when he talks to me.

'You can't have my phone, but you can look at it,' I say, my hand quivering as I hold it out to show him. 'Here's the map, look. That's where we're going now. FNC – it stands for fish 'n' chips. It's meant to be super-cool.'

Daniel grips the phone, staring at the screen intently.

We're in the middle of the entrance to the tube station. Mum and Dad are arguing about the best way to get to this restaurant. Grandma's telling a homeless person all about how he should just *seize the day* and *go and grab life by the ears*, but I think the homeless person just needs some money.

Daniel doesn't reply to me, but I want to keep him with me for as long as I can so I carry on talking: 'And look – the second red arrow is tomorrow's chip shop. It's only twenty minutes' walk from today's one, but Dad says we can stay in another hotel tonight – outside the city, near where we left the car – and come back in for lunch. Maybe go on the London Eye or something.'

Still nothing, but at least he seems to be paying attention, his finger hovering over the map, pointing from one red arrow to the other, then at the pulsing blue dot that shows where we are.

I keep going. 'Now tomorrow's chip shop is *really* special. It's the best one in the whole country AND it just happens to be the one...'

'Phone,' says Daniel, frowning and pulling the phone towards himself.

'No. That's *my* phone. I'd rather give you my arm.'

And he looks at me with heart-melting deep brown puppy-dog eyes and my fingers loosen and I hear myself saying, 'All right. All right. But look after it, OK?'

Of course Daniel doesn't say thank you. He waggles my phone in front of Monkey's face, then clutches both of them tightly to his chest.

Daniel and Monkey

— Ah, man, you're the best. We got ourselves a map. We can go anywhere, right? says Monkey.

But I'm not sure I want to go ANYWHERE. Most of all I want chips. And I now that I can't see the girl called Megan's face any more, it's sad and I miss her and everything feels a bit Grey and smoky.

Megan

We're at FNC. What a place!

We came in down some narrow stairs, and now we're in a long, narrow, low-ceilinged cellar. It's dark and busy, and decorated with all sorts of weird stuff. There are fishing nets stretched right across the ceiling. They hold up dim orange lights, which are actually buoys with bulbs inside them.

The walls are filled with huge colourful pictures. When you get close up to them you can see that they're collages – a giant jellyfish made out of plastic bags, a bucket and spade made from multicoloured flip-flops, a mosaic of a crashing wave using broken glass and pieces of shell.

The man behind the front desk is about the size of a bear. His enormous quiff brushes against the nets on the ceiling. His ears are pierced and stretched with those earrings that look like dinner plates, and there are tattoos from his fingertips all the way up to his chin.

He's wearing a super-tight sailor's uniform, including a cap and a tiny pair of white shorts that would probably be small on Daniel.

'Are you sure this is a fish and chip shop?' says Grandma.

The man behind the counter twizzles his huge

moustache. 'Er . . . no,' he says, like he feels sorry for us. 'We are, like, an experimental collective of food artists and creatives, challenging the concept of fish and chips in a unique environment.'

'What is this nutter on about?' asks Grandma. 'Can we get fish and chips here or not?'

The bear-man nods his huge head. 'Totally. Or at least, we can support you while you explore the question: *What are fish and chips?*'

Grandma rolls her eyes. 'I already know what fish and chips are. That's why I've come to a blinking fish and chip shop.'

Daniel is looking around, goggle-eyed. I'm not sure if he's excited or freaked out.

'I am your customer-experience enabler and my name is Spruce.'

'Bruce?' says Dad.

The man looks cross. 'No. Spruce. Like the tree.'

'Spruce?!' says Grandma. 'By heavens. Sounds like the stuff I spray on my athlete's foot.'

Spruce leads us to a table.

Well, I say 'table'. The tabletop is made up of rough planks of wood of all different lengths. The legs are completely random: a broken rowing oar, two multicoloured Lego towers and (I'm not joking) a false leg. The chairs are just as mismatched – three wonky stools, an old wheelchair and a really uncomfortable-looking camping chair with the seat made out of fishing net.

'What would the Major make of this place, eh?' asks Grandma.

Spruce waves his hand. 'All the objects you see here are things that've been washed up on beaches. Even the materials we used to make the art on the walls.'

'You don't say,' says Grandma, picking up the creepy doll's-head-candleholder in the middle of the table and putting it down again. I look around – all of the furniture at the other tables is similarly irregular.

'The Lego is my favourite,' says Spruce. 'Two hundred thousand pieces floated ashore in Kent from a sunken container ship. Five of us went down with a van and foraged enough for half the table legs in the restaurant.'

Daniel strokes a Lego table leg with his finger. I feel a little tug in my stomach. He used to love Lego. He'd never mix the colours up like this though.

We sit down. Grandma unclips her bumbag and dumps it on the table with a thud.

'I love your bumbag,' gushes Spruce. 'It really makes a statement.'

'Such as: *I'm a massive bumbag,*' says Dad.

I'm the only person who laughs.

'Do you have a menu?' asks Mum. It's the first thing she's said since we got here. I get the feeling she wants this to be over and done with as soon as possible.

'We believe that a menu is like a prison to creativity,' says Spruce. 'We encourage our chefs to express themselves artistically, then we bring the results to you.'

'And how do we know how much to pay?' asks Dad, looking worried.

Spruce purses his lips. 'Our food-enjoyers pay only what they feel the meal is worth.'

Dad nods. I can tell he thinks he'll be able to get away with only spending a pound or two. 'Well, that sounds grea—'

'Ts and Cs apply,' interrupts Spruce. 'Minimum spend forty pounds per person, not including drinks and tips. Extra charges may apply.'

'Forty quid?!' yelps Dad. 'Each?'

Every single other person in the restaurant turns to face him with a rustle of beard hair and flannel shirts. It obviously isn't cool here to squawk about how much the meal is going to cost.

'I'll pay,' says Grandma. *Twice in two days.* 'We're seizing the day. Even if this place is a flaming nuthouse.'

'Cool,' says Spruce, before disappearing.

'You must be happy to be back here in London, right, Karen?' Dad asks Mum.

Mum looks down at the table and doesn't reply.

'Your mum used to come to the market near here to

get all her crazy clothes and multicoloured hair dye,' Dad says.

'I'm here,' says Mum, not looking up, 'because you made me come here. And I'd rather not think about the old days, thanks.'

'Oh, come on,' says Dad, clapping his hands together. 'We might as well have fun. London . . . fish and chips . . . If it wasn't for fish and chips . . .'

'We'd have never been born,' I finish.

'Been born,' says Daniel, a moment after me.

Daniel and Monkey

– Yo! What was that? Been born? Why are ya talkin' to them clowns again, huh? says Monkey, ANGRY.

– I . . . I . . . don't know, I say, all SPLUTTERY. And I don't know why I said it, but I could see the coloured blocks which are LEGO and that REMINDED ME of something and I could hear the people talking WAARK WAARK WAARK and then the man said something about FISH AND CHIPS and, FOR ONE MOMENT, all of the faces appeared even though Monkey was still in my hand. And then I remembered something about BEING BORN

and so I said it out loud. But now I am confused
again because WHERE DID I REMEMBER THAT
FROM?

Just then, someone puts a CARDBOARD TRAY in
front of me and it smells DING-DANG-DELICIOUS
of fish and chips.

And now Monkey is cross and he stands on
the table right in front of me with his hands on
his hips and he says, Daniel? Daniel! Yo. Are you
listening to me? Man, this is why we gotta do
something. This is why we gotta get outta here.
They're brainwashin' ya an—

But before he can explain, a hand pulls him off
me and I can't stop it or maybe I just don't want
to.

Megan

He spoke to us again, but then he immediately stopped
and started chirping away at Monkey instead.

'I've had enough of this,' says Grandma.

She snatches Monkey off Daniel and unzips her bumbag.
I get another glimpse of that pink-and-yellow thing I saw
the other day. Before I can think where I know it from, she's

shoved Monkey into the bumbag, zipped it up and dusted her hands off. 'Done.'

You can feel everybody becoming tense. Daniel had been getting really agitated with Monkey before Grandma pulled it off him. What's he going to do now? Will he freak out? Will he get violent? Will he just cry?

His eyes begin to flick around the room. I can see his chest rising and falling quickly and he's biting his bottom lip, like he's properly seeing his surroundings for the first time. Before the accident, this kind of place would have been nightmarish for him – too much going on, too many unfamiliar things.

Now he's folding his hands over each other and biting his lips and you can see him becoming more and more jumpy. I'm scared he's going to have a full-on panic attack. Part of me wants to get Monkey out for him. It'd soothe him immediately. But we can't do that. We can't. We have to risk it. If we're going to get him back, we need to put up with his moods. We need to calm him down ourselves.

Mum goes to say something. She's always been amazing at calming him down – so's Dad, of course – but I'm next to him and I have a feeling I'll be best for him right now.

'It's OK, Snotface,' I whisper to him. 'I know it's scary, but we're all here with you. The whole family. Together. Look. There's Lego here too. And in this box there's amazing fish and chips. I promise.'

Mum gives me a reassuring look.

It's working. You can see him slowly and visibly calming down. This is incredible.

He strokes the Lego table leg up and down, up and down, moaning softly. I slide his cardboard tray right in front of his face.

Daniel

I was getting really DARK PURPLE because the room is weird and I didn't have Monkey. But then the girl called Megan started talking to me. I felt bad about Monkey struggling in the bag, but Megan's voice is nice and so is the SMELL and, come to think of it, maybe MONKEY can have a nice snooze in there while I eat because he is all SAFE and ZIPPED UP.

And I smell the SCRUMPTIOUS-SMELLING FOOD and I look at the faces, which are a bit CONFUSING. The people look FRIENDLY but they are also biting their lips and leaning forward and frowning which someone once explained might mean Orange worried as well.

But I try not to get Orange myself. And seeing

the man and the Lego gives me a HAPPY picture in my head of making something out of Lego but I don't know what. And now the White is all over me, like when you put on FRESH UNDERPANTS and that food REALLY DOES SMELL GOOD so I should probably EAT it.

Megan

Daniel reaches for the food. Everyone looks at each other, relieved.

'Well, let's see what the second-best chips in Britain taste like, shall we?' says Dad.

'I just hope Sploosh or Puce or Puke or whatever his name is hasn't had anything to do with making them,' says Grandma.

And so we open our trays.

Inside mine, I find the following things:
- a very small blown-up balloon, sealed with a peg, with 'Release me and sniff' written on it
- a toy rubber seagull
- a pile of hot, fat chips
- a beautifully gnarled-up hunk of battered fish
- a little glass of ketchup with a sign saying 'Drink me'

– a tiny green glass bottle with a cork.

'Well, I suppose it *does* look quite interesting,' says Mum, reluctantly.

'OK. Let's have a bash then,' says Dad. 'What did the article I stuck in Daniel's notebook say? *Prepare to have your minds – and taste buds – blown.*'

When you take the peg off the balloon, this steam billows out of it. It smells EXACTLY like the seaside – all salty and sharp. It's amazing.

'Chips chips chips!' says Daniel, flapping his hands from side to side. It's what he always used to do when he was excited. It's so lovely to see!

'Look,' says Dad. 'It's working! Sensory stimulation. Exactly like the doctor said.'

'We'll see,' says Mum.

I pick up the little rubber seagull and a white splodge squirts out of its bum all over my chips.

What the . . . ?

Daniel finds this pretty much the funniest thing that's ever happened, and soon he's squirting his everywhere, laughing his head off.

'Oooh, I *dream* of having a movement as soft as that,' says Grandma.

'Absolutely unnecessary,' I say, but I'm still happy. Daniel's laughing. We've separated him from Monkey. We've got amazing food to eat.

I shove a chip in my mouth. It's perfect – that little crunch of skin that gives way to the melt-in-your-mouth potato inside and . . .

Then the taste hits me.

'Urgh!' I say.

It's disgusting.

Like cardboard soaked in dirty water.

At almost the exact same moment, everyone else seems to feel the same way. Mum's scraping at her tongue. Grandma's spitting into a hanky.

'Whatever you do, don't eat the seagull-poo mayonnaise,' says Dad, gagging. 'It tastes like it might actually *be* seagull poo.'

Mum shudders. 'And that fish is *off.*'

'Waiter!' barks Grandma, rapping her stick against the floor. 'What on earth is this muck?'

Spruce reappears by the side of the table. 'Today we have lavender-and-turnip chips, with a liquefied crab-meat mayonnaise,' he says in an *isn't it obvious* kind of voice.

'I thought this was a fish and chip shop,' says Dad.

Spruce laughs without humour. 'Er, no, sir. We are an experimental collective of food artists and creatives, challenging the con—'

'We've heard this before,' interrupts Dad.

'And what's the rest of it then?' asks Grandma.

Spruce tuts impatiently, then points at each item in

turn. 'The *fish* is actually flakes of freeze-dried octopus throat in a cauliflower crust.'

'Octopus *what*?' squeals Grandma.

Spruce tuts again, as if he's never spoken to dumber people in his life. 'It's actually, like, a delicacy on certain Pacific islands.'

'What's the stuff in the glass that looks like ketchup then? Mushed-up whale testicles?' asks Dad.

Mum slaps his arm. 'Jim.'

'No. Obviously not,' says Spruce. 'We weren't allowed to use them. It's actually a shot of salt water and seaweed cordial with a hint of starfish blood. And the green bottle contains the stomach juices of a squid.'

'Good grief,' says Grandma.

'We are here to support you while you explore the deconstructed concept of fish and chips,' says Spruce.

We've heard this before too. On another table, I can hear a waiter tell his customers that they are *pushing the boundaries of the dining experience*. It's like the headquarters of a flipping cult.

I turn to Daniel.

The laughter has disappeared. He's pressing his fingers into his ears and rocking back and forth. A little ball of half-chewed food is on the table in front of him, the rest of his chips scattered about where he's smacked the box away from himself. He's moaning horribly.

I can imagine that this would be the worst thing in the world for him – stuff that looks like fish and chips but isn't. It's all too much for his brain to handle and now he's clawing at his eyes and grinding his teeth.

What were we thinking?

And what did the doctor say? Since the accident he can't trust the world any more. Now we've done *this* to him! We've given him his favourite thing, then used it to trick him. How stupid can you get?

'Quick!' I say. And I don't want to say this next bit but I know it's the only thing that'll work: 'We need to calm him down. Get Monkey.'

Grandma grabs her bumbag and fumbles with the zip. She tries to pull Monkey out, but he won't come so I snatch the bumbag off her and tip the contents onto the table. Boiled sweets and coins and old tissues come raining out, along with Monkey.

Daniel clutches it to his chest quickly and starts crying into it.

But then his eyes open wide and he screams.

There's something else on the table.

And I suddenly realise what the yellow-and-pink thing I saw in there before is.

Daniel and Monkey

— Look! Look at that! On the table! Look what they got there! I told ya they were a bunch o' creeps! Monkey cries, and he is PANTING and CLUTCHING HIS NECK because he can't BREATHE.

I look at the table but I can't believe it.

Lying right there is MONKEY'S TAIL.

His TAIL!

— We gotta get outta here. They stole my tail, man. C'mon!

And my brain is going SUPER-FIZZY, like a Blue and an Orange and a Red all at once because there is Monkey's tail. Why do they have his tail?

But there is ANOTHER THING that's making me go SPINNY and that is the way the CHIPS are scattered across the table with MONKEY'S TAIL lying next to them. It makes me think of something else. Something horrible that makes me feel SICK and FROZEN to the spot.

— Whatcha waitin' for? Grab the tail. And make sure you got the phone.

I don't know what to do because NOW the PICTURE is in my head again — the PICTURE of the

LIGHTS. The *SCREECH*. The PAIN.

— Fix up, man. They're evil! We gotta go! NOW!

And I don't know what I'm doing, but Monkey SNATCHES up his tail and YANKS me away and we STAGGER to a door with a green sign over the top and we SLAM against a bar and up some steps and a siren goes off but I do not care. We are OUTSIDE.

Megan

We chase after him, tripping over tables and bumping into waiters, the alarm screeching across the room. When we reach the fire door, Spruce has already closed it so I try to squeeze round him to reach the handle but he blocks my path.

'Fire door only,' he says.

'Get out the way!' I snap.

'There are health and safe— YEOW!'

Grandma's next to me and she's jabbed him in the toes with her stick, and he hops on one foot and squeals with pain and now the four of us have tumbled up some concrete steps and onto the pavement but it's busy with people – jostling crowding people – and it's dark apart

228

from the pools of street light and we look left, look right, but he's nowhere to be seen.

There's a horrible dragging feeling in my belly.

He's gone.

Daniel and Monkey

I'm running with Monkey, dodging between people, and we cross the road then run down another road then round a tight corner.

— This is PERFECT! says Monkey and he sounds Blue excited.

— What do you MEAN? I ask. I don't understand why he is excited because I am still a big shaken-up bottle of ORANGE RED BLUE Coca-Cola.

— At last! We're free of them schmucks! 's what we always wanted, ain't it?

And I wail loud and fall against a wall because I don't know if it IS what I wanted and I don't know what I want. I am SCARED of the people who stole Monkey's tail and I am SCARED on my own with Monkey in the big city and I am SCARED because of WHAT I THOUGHT OF when I saw MONKEY'S TAIL and the SCATTERED CHIPS and I don't know what to do and it feels nice when I press my head against the cold bricks.

— Hey. Don't give up on me, big guy. We're on our own now. Just the two of us.

And someone has their hand on my back and they say, Are you OK? And I howl and run away again.

Now my feet are SLAPPING on the pavement and I am CRASHING past people and I don't know what to do. Don't know where to go. And then I remember the PHONE and I look at it and I see the BLUE GLOWING DOT which is us but on the map. Then I see the RED ARROW and I RUN TOWARDS IT because it's the only place I can think of.

— Hey. Where we goin'? asks Monkey, but I don't answer him.

Your Guide to the Best Fish and Chip Shops in the UK

1) Bill's Chip Van, Near King's Cross, London

Always parked just a few minutes' walk from King's Cross Station, Bill's Chip Van is one of London's hidden gems. A long-standing favourite with students at the nearby art college, Bill offers street food at its very best – affordable, generous and very, VERY tasty.

Megan

Dad and I run one way, Mum and Grandma the other. Yelling his name. Standing on tiptoes. Craning our necks. There's nothing, just a river of people flowing along the pavements. This is impossible. I head back.

Mum's crying and fretting. 'I knew something like this would happen.'

Then I realise something.

'Wait,' I say, and it's suddenly so obvious that my heart just flutters. 'Dad. He's got my phone.'

'So?'

'Location sharing! You and Mum have got me on yours. We can find him.'

'Good thinking, Meg,' says Mum.

There isn't time to feel proud of myself. I open up the maps on Dad's phone, which seems to take forever and then finally it opens and the map appears and I zoom in and *there it is*. A glowing blue dot. *Daniel.*

Relief floods through me.

We watch it zig-zagging slowly along a road, while Dad looks around us at street signs, trying to match up which direction to follow him in.

'You two go, and we'll follow,' says Mum, who's also

fumbling with her phone. 'Just make sure you find him safe.'

Dad and I set off running down the road.

Daniel and Monkey

I'm running super-fast but my brain is working SUPER-FASTER, whizzing round so much I feel like it might EXPLODE.

I can't get the pictures out of my head — CAR LIGHTS and a SCREECHING SOUND. The CHIPS scattered on the table, like CHIPS SCATTERED ON TARMAC. And MONKEY'S TAIL right there.

I'm realising something, like when you're building something out of Lego and you slowly start to see what it's going to be when it's finished.

Ahead of me is a VAN by the road on a little square and it has lights at the side and I can see a big sign that says BILL'S CHIP VAN and I look at the phone and my little blue dot is right next to the red arrow.

— What the . . . ? French fries? Are you kiddin' me?

Megan

My lungs are burning. It's hard to run quickly on the busy pavements because of all the people, so we're cutting through some dingy side streets, which are quiet enough for us to go down the middle of the road. There's a whining noise behind us and we have to jump out of the way of a motor scooter, which weaves round us without slowing down.

We check the map. Daniel's a few streets away. At least we know he's not been bundled into a car or got completely lost. Not yet anyway.

'Come on,' Dad pants, and off we go again.

Daniel and Monkey

We are at the van with the chips and there is a man leaning down and he asks me what I want, but I don't answer him because Monkey is talking to me at the SAME TIME.

— Yo, D-Machine. This is nuts. Get outta here now. I mean it, man. That's an order.

— An order? I ask because I'm thinking that friends don't ORDER their friends around and there's a SHRIEKING PAIN in my brain and the man in the chip van asks me what I want to eat but I don't say anything to him because I've just realised something.

— You . . . you lied to me, I say.

And my brain is BROWN, which is a new feeling, when you are hollow like an old tree trunk.

— Lied? I didn't lie. Whatcha talkin' about? You're losin' it, man.

And I say, But you did. You're meant to be my friend but you lied to me. You told me YOU were run over but . . . But . . .

And in my head there's a picture. But it's not a picture, it's a MEMORY!

A real-life memory.

And it's me and I've got a bag of fish and chips and I am running across a road and there's bright lights and a loud screech and then . . .

Everything hurts and I'm awake asleep floaty falling pain and bright lights.

I SCREAM.

Megan

We stop for a second to catch our breath and look at the screen. His blue dot is right on top of the last red arrow – Bill's Chip Van. It's no longer moving. *Of course he'd go there* – the only other destination on the phone.

'We're – about – a minute – away,' says Dad, barely able to get the words out. 'Last push.'

As he says it, I hear a distant scream, and I hope with all my heart that it's not Daniel.

We set off again.

Daniel and Monkey

– Can I contact someone for you? says the Chip Van Man who I don't know.

– It was me! I was run over! I say.

And Monkey has a big angry grin on his face and he says, Yeah. You were. And that was the greatest thing that ever happened to ya.

– How CAN it be? I say because my brain is mushy peas and gravy.

And Monkey stares at me and he says, Because that was the moment I came to life.

— No!

— I'm starting to worry about you, says the Chip Shop Man.

— Ah, butt out of it, butthead, snaps Monkey.

— I'll come down, says Chip Shop Man.

— And look at ya now with them doofuses. Speakin' to 'em. Eatin' their damn French fries. That's the thanks I get for lookin' after ya after your accident.

— No, Monkey, I looked after y—

But I don't finish what I was going to say because I realise it's not true.

— Ah, buddy! I pretend like I need YOU because that makes YOU feel better. Makes ya feel important. But it's the OTHER WAY ROUND. You ain't nothin' without me. And you're tryin' to ditch me. Tryin' to ditch your old pal Monkey, aintcha?

— No, Monkey. No.

But I suddenly feel VERY TURQUOISE because maybe he might be a BIT RIGHT, because I like seeing the people, especially the girl called MEGAN, and I can't see them when Monkey is there at the same time.

The Chip Shop Man is next to me now but I can

hardly hear him talking to me.

– Well, buddy. You know what they wanna do, doncha?

– No.

– How many times do I gotta tell ya? They wanna get rid of me.

I feel like I'm standing at the top of a HIGH CLIFF. No, I say. They're nice.

– No, they ain't. Ya saw that old dame had my tail. And she locked me up in that body bag like I was already dead.

– No, Monkey.

And Monkey looks me deep in the eye. You gotta choose. It's your old pal Monkey or them filthy animals and their French fries. What's it gonna be?

Megan

'Round this corner,' says Dad. 'Yes! That's it! Just where it always was.'

And then we can see him, and the whole world is suddenly brighter. He's standing outside the chip van, Monkey right up in front of his face.

It doesn't look like the best chip shop in the country –

it's just a tatty old van, just a little bit bigger than something you'd buy an ice cream from. It's sitting on a wide corner of pavement, across from a pub and with railway arches behind. It's got a scruffy sign and a small plastic table and chairs next to the open hatch. The owner is away to the side, his back to Daniel, speaking into a mobile with his finger in his other ear. A dim light from inside spills out through the hatch onto the road.

'So that's where I met your mum,' says Dad.

'If it wasn't for fish and chips . . .' I murmur, and we head over towards Daniel.

Daniel and Monkey

Monkey's question is HANGING IN THE AIR and I WANT to say that I choose him. I really do.

But then, just as my lips are making the words, I hear something. A VOICE.

— Snotface!

And before I look across, I already know who it is. The girl called Megan. And Daddy, the man. And now a special car with a yellow light on top has stopped next to them and Mummy and Grandma, the two women, get out. And as they walk towards me, the smell of CHIPS and the sound of SIZZLING from the van seems to get stronger.

— I knew it. I knew you'd choose them, says Monkey.

— No, Monkey. It's not like that, I say, PANICKING.

— It's over, man.

— What are you doing, Monkey? I say, but even though he's only tiny, he's dragging me round the back of the van and in through an open door.

— Hey! You can't go up there! says the Chip Van Man but the door is slammed shut and locked, and I am INSIDE the chip van and it is HOT and LOUD and SIZZLY and we crawl between the seats and into the kitchen part behind.

Megan

We run round the back of the chip van, where the owner is rattling the door handle. 'He's locked me out!' he says.

'He's my son,' says Mum. 'Have you got another key?'

When the owner turns round, he looks from Mum to Dad and back again and he does a proper cartoon double-take. 'Hang on. I know you two. Karen and er . . . John. No, Jimmy. Jim. That's it. You used to have mad hair. Made me do your wedding. I remember. Only wedding I've ever done.'

'We met here,' offers Dad.

'Ah, that's really sweet,' says the owner.

And for a millisecond it crosses my mind how sweet this actually is – Dad trying to fix the family by lugging us round the country, and surprising Mum by taking us all to the place where they met. Only it hasn't quite turned out that way, and Mum doesn't seem in the slightest bit interested. And anyway, we've got way more important things to think about.

There's a thumping sound from inside the chip van.

'Keys,' says Mum, clicking her fingers. 'Quickly.'

'They're in the cab,' Bill says. 'I know – I'll stand on the table and reach through the hatch to unlock the doors.'

He runs back round the other side, just as the van starts bouncing violently. From inside we hear Daniel groaning.

'Hurry up!' shouts Mum.

'Keep calm, Big D,' says Dad through the door.

'Don't touch anything sharp,' calls Grandma. 'And grab us a tin of 7 Up if you can.'

I stand there, useless and helpless, just like on the night of his accident.

Daniel and Monkey

Monkey is trying to fight his way towards the bubbling fat, which is SUPER-HOT. I don't want to go near it, but he is too strong and I can't hold him back.

— What are you doing, Monkey? I yell at him, and I am SUPER-CONFUSED and all of my feelings are exploding out of my head in a great big MULTICOLOURED RAINBOW.

And Monkey's eyes are wild and crazy and he is panting and he says, Don't ya see it, buddy? They want me outta your life. And YOU want me outta your life too. Ya had the chance and ya chose THEM.

— No, Monkey, I don't. I need you.

— Not like I need you, D-Man. Not like I need you.

And he's trying to get closer to the fryer, which is BAD NEWS, and I can hear it sizzling and I'm on my knees now so close that little SPECKS of HOT FAT are flicking up onto my cheeks and stinging me like BURNY WASPS.

— No, Monkey! I beg, STRAINING to hold him still.

— No hard feelings. Good luck to ya, buddy.

Suddenly I can hear the voices outside. The lock clicks. The door opens. The people scramble into the van from both sides.

And Monkey looks at me and he says, I'll always love you, Daniel.

Then he dives out of my hands and into the hot fat.

I don't think. I just PLUNGE my hands in to rescue him and the pain is a BLINDING LIGHT and everything disappears.

Megan

Daniel snuffles and wriggles his head.

'Are you OK, Snotface?' I say.

He blinks a few times and looks around at the hospital room. His bandaged hands are huge bulbous paws.

'He's awake!' says Mum, scrambling out of her chair.

'It HURTS!' he whines. His voice is slow and slurred from the painkillers they've given him.

'Oh my boy. My boy,' says Dad, and he and Mum rush over and grab him round the legs.

Daniel winces and closes his eyes again. I hold my hand to my mouth, tears seeping down my cheeks.

It was chaos in the chip van.

There were cans of drink rolling round everywhere, and Dad and I were both scrambling through the narrow kitchen to get to Daniel, who was lying on the floor, passed out, hot fat dripping down his bright red arms.

Straightaway, Dad dragged Daniel across the tiny kitchen space to the sink, and I ran his hands under the cold tap. 'Call an ambulance!' howled Dad.

But Mum had already jumped in the driver's seat.

'We're borrowing the van,' said Mum, as if this was the most normal thing in the world. 'There isn't time to wait. The hospital's only five minutes away.'

'How do you know?' asked Grandma, who'd scrambled in next to her in the front.

Mum tutted. 'I lived here for three years. Jim, cover the hot fat and get that window closed.'

A funny smile spread across his face as he lay Daniel down on the floor and darted across to the hatch.

Mum started the engine. 'Megan. Find something cold.'

I understood straightaway why Dad was smiling. This wasn't my boring old Mum. This was punky, rule-breaker Mum, back from the dead.

The van lurched forward, burning hot fat almost sloshing out of the fryer as Dad struggled to pull the cover over it. We bounced off the pavement and swung a U-turn. There was the sound of splintering plastic as she crushed the table and chairs.

'What are you doing?' cried the chip van owner, diving in through the open passenger door with his legs hanging out behind him.

Grandma helped him in and he yanked the door shut as Mum bunny-hopped the van down the street.

'Saving my son,' said Mum.

'That's the woman I married!' said Dad, staggering against the cooker.

There was no way we'd be able to hold Daniel up by the sink with the van flying around like this. Struggling to stay upright as we screeched round a corner, I grabbed a plastic bag. Then I desperately filled it with fish from the fridge, trying to ignore how cold and slimy and gross it was. The van jolted, knocking me to my knees. I tied a knot in the bulging bag, wrapped it in a tea towel and carefully held it around Daniel's hands.

'Here you go, Snotface. This should be nice and cool.'

The van roared through a red light. Someone hooted their horn.

Mum lets go of Daniel and gives me a kiss on the cheek.

'What's that for?' I say. Normally I feel too old for kisses from Mum, but this one was really nice.

'You were so clever with the fish,' she whispers into my ear. 'You know, the doctor said you might've saved him from serious scarring.'

I beam so much I think my cheeks will burst.

A nurse comes into the room. 'How's the patient?'

Daniel squints at her.

'He spoke a minute ago,' says Dad. 'Said it hurts.'

The nurse puts her hand on Daniel's forehead. 'It will do. We'll sort out the dose of his painkillers when he wakes up properly.'

'Monkey?' Daniel croaks, then his eyes close and he drifts off to sleep again. I'm kind of glad he's only half-conscious. I don't think he'd be able to handle being in hospital.

I take Monkey out of the little sink in the corner of the room where I've been scrubbing it, and I dry it on the roll of blue paper towel. It's wet and a bit foamy with hand soap, which was the best I could find, and its T-shirt and fur are all yellow from the fryer. When you squeeze it, oil oozes out of the hole above its bum. I wrap it in paper towel and place it on Daniel's chest.

'It'll need to go in the washing machine,' says Mum.

Grandma reaches into her bumbag and pulls out Monkey's tail. 'I feel rotten about this, y'know.'

'Where did you get it from?' I say.

Grandma sighs. 'I suppose I picked it up after the accident and shoved it in my bumbag for safekeeping. There's so much in there, and we were so worried about young Daniel, that I must've forgotten all about it.'

'Not to worry,' says Dad. 'He's on the mend now.'

I look at Mum, stroking Daniel's hand, then at Dad. He's got one arm round Mum and one round me, and he's smiling at Grandma.

Maybe we're all on the mend.

Mend.

Of course.

Daniel

— Monkey? I say, opening my eyes and blinking.

But Monkey doesn't answer me.

I pat my tummy. He was there a second ago but now he's gone. I groan and close my eyes again.

Megan

I rush out of the room. 'Excuse me,' I say.

The nurse looks up from the form she's filling in. 'Yes?'

'Look. I know you're probably mega-busy and everything, but can you do stitches?'

'Oh goodness! Have you cut yourself? I'll have a look, but you'll be best off down in A & E.'

'No, no, no! I want to fix this. For my brother,' I say, holding up Monkey and his tail.

The nurse nods her head kindly. 'I've got a break in half an hour. I'll see what I can do.'

I thank her and skip back, but after a few steps, I stop and turn to her again. 'Actually, can you just lend me a needle and thread?'

She raises her eyebrows.

'I think it's important that I do it,' I explain, even though I'm not sure why.

'Do you mind if I help you, Meg?' says Mum, who must've been standing right behind me.

I turn around and give her the biggest hug of all time.

Daniel and Monkey

I open my eyes and Monkey is back on my tummy
again!

— Monkey! I say, all pink and happy.

He doesn't say anything.

His eyes don't move behind his black glasses.

I grab his hand and he just flops forward onto
my belly.

— Oh no! Monkey! What's wrong? I cry.

And THAT'S when I notice HIS TAIL.

It's back on him, GOOD AS NEW!

— You've been FIXED! It looks amazing! I say.

But Monkey doesn't answer me.

— Monkey? I say. And I shake him and stroke his
face but he STILL doesn't reply.

And I SUDDENLY UNDERSTAND.

And even though I'm so happy that Monkey has
been mended, there's a BIG SCRATCHY LUMP in my
throat like a coconut.

I know that he's not going to answer me. I know
that he's just a toy.

I kiss Monkey's hand, which tastes a bit like

chips, and I say, I love you, Monkey. And I'll keep you with me forever.

Megan

Daniel's sucking Monkey's hand, which must be disgusting after it's been in the fryer. A little tear rolls down the side of his face but I can tell he's happy.

Then, just as he looks like he's beginning to notice where he is, the nurse from before comes in, holding a carrier bag. 'Oooh! Nice work on the stitches,' she says, examining Monkey's tail. 'You'll be after my job next.'

I smile at Mum and she wrinkles her nose back at me.

The nurse puts the bag on the table by Daniel's bed. 'Somebody called Bill dropped these in reception for you. Just don't let the doctors catch you eating them in here.'

She winks at us, then leaves.

'Chips! Chips! CHIPS!' says Daniel, sitting up in bed and pretending to clap his massive bulbous paws together. It seems as if the food's distracted him from the strangeness of being in hospital. For now at least.

We all burst out laughing and Dad starts doling out the chips. Immediately, the room fills with swirling steam that settles on the monitors next to Daniel's bed and blurs the screens.

Oh! I'm starving! Give me extra!

What's in that pot? Curry sauce! Oh yes! Pour some on mine!

Hey! Not all of it!

Battered sausage? I'll split it with you. Yum yum!

Hold on! I'm doing it!

Proper ketchup! Lovely job!

And now we're sitting around Daniel's bed, Dad and I perched on the end, Mum and Grandma on the visitors' chairs.

'So good!' I say. Warmth and happiness and family are flooding through me. I break off a crispy chunk of battered fish, dip it in tomato sauce and pass it into Daniel's mouth. Eyes closed, he savours every chew of it.

'Bill's Chip Van! I'd forgotten how good it was,' says Mum.

Dad groans. 'I hadn't. The taste of the chips! Takes me back to that night I met you.'

Mum tilts her head and smiles. 'Thanks for taking us back there.'

'I wanted it to be a surprise,' says Dad. 'If it wasn't for fish and chips . . .'

'We'd have never been born,' says everyone at the same time.

Mum kisses Dad on the lips, and Daniel winks at me and puts his big, fat, bandaged hand towards his mouth. He pretends to throw up and I feel myself start to sob. Now we're all sobbing, except Daniel, who's licking his lips in the way that always used to make them go red. 'More, Megan! More!'

'Calm down, Snotface,' I say, wiping my tears away and laughing. Then I pick out the biggest, juiciest chip from the tray and pop it into his mouth.

The End

NOTES ON DANIEL

Daniel's position on the autistic spectrum is perhaps a little different from the presentation we usually encounter in books and films, i.e. the highly advanced maths whizz who struggles with personal relationships.

I don't pretend to be an expert on autism but I've worked with many autistic children during my teaching career, and I understand it to be an extremely broad and diverse condition. For instance, contrary to what we normally see in popular culture, plenty of autistic children I've taught have found maths extremely challenging (and not just because they've had me as a teacher!).

My approach in the classroom is that – while labels and diagnoses can be useful to a certain extent – we should always treat each child as a unique individual. In Daniel I've tried to create a character who is shaped by certain traits of autism, but who isn't a stereotypical 'autistic character'.

In the book, Daniel, links his moods to colours. This

is something I've seen used in classrooms with varying degrees of success (again, depending on the needs of the individual child). Like Megan, I'm not sure if he actually sees the colours or if it's simply a way of him clarifying and understanding his emotions. For reference, here's the list I used when I was writing the book:

Red – angry
Black – uncontrollably angry
Orange – worried or scared
Blue – over-excited
Green – silly
Brown – hollow and empty
Grey – sad
Pink – extremely happy
White – calm
Purple – nervous or tense
Turquoise – guilty
Yellow – confused

ACKNOWLEDGEMENTS

I've had a lot of help writing this book, so I'd like to say thank you to:

– Professor Barry Wright (University of York, and Leeds and York NHS Partnership Foundation Trust) and my wonderful sister-in-law Dr Rachel Lancaster, who gave invaluable advice about Daniel's presentation which shaped the whole book.

– Donna Lynn Shepherd (from the inspirational Arc School in Ansley), Julie Aspin and Rachel Lancaster (again), who cast their eyes over a later draft and offered perceptive comments from different viewpoints, and who also gave me powerful insights into autism and its effect on families.

– The team at Piccadilly Press and especially my editor, Georgia Murray, who has been patient and supportive throughout the three million drafts I've sent to her, and has made countless improvements and suggestions along the way. Also Talya Baker, who had the great idea of using chip cones as section breaks. All the mistakes are mine!

– Gillie Russell, who I'm so proud and lucky to have as my agent, advisor, sounding board, agony aunt and friend.

– My dear old dad, who sadly passed away this year, and who taught me everything I know about telling stories. And my mum for being there always (MrsMaryWoodcock might be named after you, but her appearance was pure fiction, Mum, I promise).

– Most of all, my family, for everything else.

ALSO BY MARK LOWERY

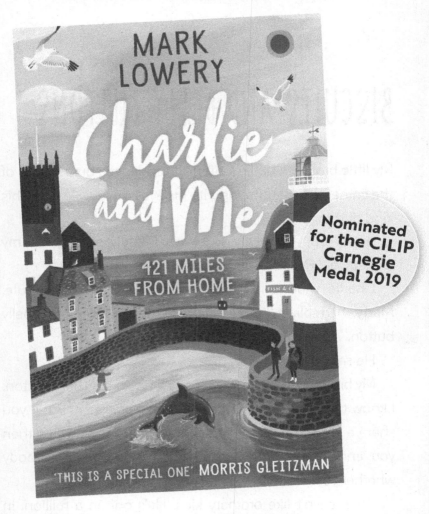

MARK LOWERY

Charlie and Me

421 MILES FROM HOME

Nominated for the CILIP Carnegie Medal 2019

'THIS IS A SPECIAL ONE' MORRIS GLEITZMAN

TURN THE PAGE TO READ AN EXTRACT . . .

Piccadilly
PRESS

BISCUITS AND BELLY BUTTONS

My little brother Charlie's sitting cross-legged on the floor of the corner shop, humming with his eyes closed. He does this kind of thing a lot.

'Hurry up,' I say, giving him a friendly shove with my raggedy old Reebok. 'We've got a train to catch.'

Charlie wipes his nose on his sleeve. 'Gizza minute, Marty,' he replies. 'I'm just charging up the laser in my belly button.'

He *says* this kind of thing a lot too.

My brother Charlie doesn't have a laser in his belly button. I know this for a fact. Not that I've ever *studied* it. But if you share a small bedroom with your brother for ten years then you end up pretty well acquainted with his whole body whether you like it or not.

Charlie isn't like ordinary kids. He's one in a million. In fact, he's one in a *Charlillion*. A Charlillion, by the way, is a number he invented, which is one more than infinity. I tried to explain to him that you can't have one more than infinity. Infinity means it goes on forever. Charlie called me a banana-brain. He can be very childish when he wants to be.

At poetry club in school, Mr Hendrix sometimes plays a game to warm up. You've got to talk about a topic for thirty seconds without stopping or repeating yourself. Here's what I'd say about Charlie:

'Lazy eye, massive head, snores like a hippo, often ill, weird taste in food, terrible memory, always out of breath cos of his asthma, weedy, cheeky, can't do anything for himself or concentrate for more than two seconds, brain's inside out, no understanding of danger. My absolute best mate in the whole entire world.'

I'd have to stop there. You could talk about Charlie for a Charlillion seconds if you wanted to, and you'd never run out of things to say.

'Which biscuits do you fancy?' I ask him. Mr Farook is watching us carefully from behind the counter. Each time I glance over he's there, leaning right back so he can see along the aisle. I smile at him but his face stays blank. I'm starting to feel queasy.

Charlie pushes his milk-bottle specs up on his nose and squints at me through his lazy eye. His good eye has a Peppa Pig patch on it so that his lazy one learns to work harder. *Peppa Pig* is one of Charlie's favourite shows, despite him being at least six years older than the average viewer. 'Why can't we have one of the biscuits from your rucksack?'

I clutch the rucksack to my chest, squeezing the hard corners of the omni-special-leftover-from-Christmas biscuit tin that I pinched from home. Of course Charlie saw me nick the biscuits. He sees everything, even though his eyes are rubbish. Maybe he's not got a laser in his belly button. Maybe it's a CCTV camera.

'They're special,' I say. 'They're for when we get there.'

'Get where?'

'Where we're going.'

I don't want to tell him where we're going till we're on the train. He'll only get excited. And trust me, an excited Charlie is not what I need in my life at quarter to seven on a Saturday morning. Imagine filling a puppy with blue Smarties and Lemon Fanta, then bouncing it on a trampoline: that's Charlie when he's excited.

'Are there any of those chocolate wheels in the tin?' he asks.

'Course,' I say.

'What about the hefty thick ones in the golden foil? They're my favourites. Ninety per cent chocolate. Five per cent biscuit.'

'What's the other five per cent?' I ask, just because he's always got a weird answer.

Charlie sniffs hard. 'Dreams.'

Told you. Brain inside out.

He settles on a packet of Jammy Dodgers from the shelf (an excellent choice) and we go to pay.

When I get my wallet out I accidentally flash my wad of twenty-pound notes, which is a mistake. Mr Farook's big furry eyebrows shoot up his forehead. The guy's like a bloodhound for money. The police should use him to sniff out where gangsters hide their cash.

'Going somewhere special?' he says, nodding at my rucksack.

I'm trying to figure out how to answer this when Charlie butts in.

'Switzerland,' he says seriously. 'I'm getting my belly-button laser upgraded.'

By the time Mr Farook can reply, we're out on the street.

'Nice work, boss,' I say, giving Charlie a fist-bump. He gives me his cheekiest, squintiest, one-eyed grin and we set off walking to the train station.